THE ROMANTIC PHENOMENON OF JIMMY PAGE

Juliann White

MINERVA PRESS

LONDON
MIAMI DELHI SYDNEY

THE ROMANTIC PHENOMENON OF JIMMY PAGE
Copyright © Juliann White 1999

All Rights Reserved

ISBN 0 75410 958 5

First Published 1999 by
MINERVA PRESS
315–317 Regent Street
London W1R 7YB

Printed in Great Britain for Minerva Press

THE ROMANTIC PHENOMENON OF JIMMY PAGE

Contents

Introduction

When the world population was increasing dramatically as a result of the baby boom of 1945–1964, musical styles were beginning a period of diversification the like of which had never been seen before. The majority of young people of this period were mysteriously united in their boredom with traditional institutions because they were not meeting their needs for rewarding work and social justice. We live in a world of governments, but musicians of this time were not dictated to by a ruling class. Self-indulgence played a large role in their search for accomplishing the objectives of creating a happier, peaceful and more loving world. William Blake's philosophy of: 'The road of excess leads to the palace of wisdom' captures the general idea.

People not only need each other, but they also care about and love each other. Musicians have a perfect forum for reaching out to many. Music listening can be a social experience and the healing power of music is ideal for people when they are commuting in cars, relaxing, studying and working. Listening to Baroque music can improve the human ability to memorise and concentrate, some music can lower or raise blood pressure, increase pain-killing endorphins and relieve the pain of headaches. Since we are no longer bound to the land or religion for survival we are lacking without some sort of soulful sustenance. Music has been this for me and many of my friends during my lifetime.

The Restoration of the 1660s in England, the Enlightenment of the 1760s in Europe, the Civil War of the 1860s in America and the US involvement in the Viet Nam War in the 1960s were similar periods in the people's rejection of accepted social institutions and the goal of some was to improve and stabilise these societies. Jimmy Page developed directly during this latter reformative era; he then instituted a sublime art form within the context of modern technology. This writing is meant to be an explanation of the genius with which he created.

Entertainers of the 1960s were considered shocking if they shook on stage or if they wore their hair shaggy. Earlier performers were well liked when they were clean and well dressed in public, whereas, after the British mods, many performers of the 1960s began to bring filth and dishevelment into vogue. Eroticism slowly began to enter the musical performer's act. During this time Page was getting his musical chops up and becoming quite familiar with the American blues players' techniques which would be invaluable to him when the time came for him to create his own sound.

My inspiration to write came to me when I was fourteen years of age and as a result of my isolated life at a Catholic boarding school called the Home of the Good Shepherd. I wrote religious poetry until I entered university in 1990. I began to play guitar in 1978 as a result of a friendship I had with a girl who played very well. I practised and played diligently for ten years, probably because it gave me an avenue for expressing my written lyrics. For me, guitar playing was always work, I never really enjoyed it in the same way I do writing. I quit playing guitar in 1988 because I knew I would never create the kind of transcendental and Romantic music played by Jimmy Page. Upon quitting music I began to define what it was that endowed him with his remarkable musical abilities. I have narrowed this down to four basic factors: first his being an only child. I am also an only child so I know and remember as a child and adolescent being allowed continuous, free time to express myself creatively without having to argue or compete with any siblings. Second, being raised in England with its rich, historical heritage and a bevy of creative artists who gave so generously during the centuries which led up to the twentieth. Third, a determination to succeed combined with a horrifying fear of poverty and an absolute negligence of negative thinking combined with a cautious and realistic nature. Fourth, and possibly the most important factor in breeding the innocuous proclivity Page had toward playing music forever was his natural ability to put himself in the right place at the right time with the best people to further his goals. An ability to cast off his inhibitions developed over the years and was reflected in the performance I saw at the MGM Grand Garden on the exact date of my graduation from university, 12th May, 1995.

Recently, I had the misfortune of hearing a guitarist of a non-consequential band on Rockline, a radio show, poke fun at Jimmy Page for being inarticulate on one occasion. I immediately began to think: perhaps that *is* so, but without the presence of Page on the planet you would never have had a market place for your derivative and ordinary brand of loud, irritating and meaningless music. Page played loud, heavy, blues which was partially influenced by his constant exposure to loud sounds from the Heathrow airport community in which he spent much time as a child. After the demise of Page's band, Led Zeppelin, in 1980, heavy, innovative blues music went in a very lacklustre direction. While blues music will never die, the Romantic blues genre played by Led Zeppelin has only since been played by Jimmy Page. An appeal to natural, but undefinable human feelings is made in the song 'Black Dog'. The hunger and desperation for human warmth is felt in 'Shake My Tree' from the *Coverdale Page* CD. This refined elegance in a furiously, transcendent style is only done in rock bands in which Jimmy Page plays. This music I love always has a heated, hurried pace and in the lyrics are found references to burning, waiting, dying and other important world events. The sound of the loud, heavy blues he played became instantly recognisable in what was commonly known as heavy metal music throughout the 1980s. This genre, symbolic of intensity, carries with it enormous potential to encapsulate great beauty and strong emotions as the vocals of Robert Plant and the music of Jimmy Page both demonstrate. Available to the expert guitarist is a vast realm in which to showcase expertise which is what James Patrick Page has done.

As I have developed this book I have become aware of the mechanics of the music business and the events which have led to a surplus of electric guitarists, of which I will show how Jimi Hendrix and Jimmy Page are the most remarkable and have been the most influential. My favourite music came from the heart and soul of Jimmy Page, who lived much longer than Hendrix, created a larger body of work and who toured the United States in 1995 when I saw him in concert. In the following pages I tell what I feel to be most relevant about Jimmy Page as an artist. My generation followed his and mine is the generation of people who never thought they would see Jimmy Page perform live, because of the demise of Led Zeppelin, but by some miracle he personally gifted us with the music.

Sustain

The soul of wisdom is the knowledge of and acknowledgement of the Supreme Being.[1]

Emmanuel Swedenborg

Whenever I listen to music by Beethoven or Led Zeppelin or I read literature in the genre of *Frankenstein* by Mary Shelley (1818) I feel the depths of the dark, blue Mediterranean Sea I saw in Vientimilla, Italy and these are the feelings I need to live my life. Fast, hard and frightening like the rhythm of life. When in doubt climb a mountain. Writing books and playing music are both human attempts at reaching God. The Romantic movement in literature places a fondness for nature at its forefront. Embodying human imagination and emotion as well as the environmental landscape and beginning at the eighteenth century it is best expressed in English and American poetry and in *Walden, Or Life in the Woods* by Henry David Thoreau (1854). Always containing a melancholy tone and a sense of independent rebellion, Romantic literature and poetry is deep and contemplative, lonely and unconcerned with rigid structure or rhyme scheme.

The intrinsic connection between the political literary and social climate in the world and the aspirations and works of great artists is visible when viewed simultaneously with the culture in which they work and grow. Important

Southern-American novelist William Faulkner's description of art in general thought that it should show the conflict within the human heart. Popular music nearly always reflects this type of sentiment. Romantic music merely glimpses purity, sweetness and light; however, these are present in an earthy degree.

Beginning with Ludwig van Beethoven we have it all; from his lengthened scherzo to his sonata, there are present the light and jocular and the warm though secretive feelings found naturally in human interaction. He created nine symphonies, sixteen quartets, thirty-two piano sonatas and in his hymns, marches and overtures he captured all natural beauty. Beethoven's 'Ninth Symphony' began the Romantic era and it introduced the human voice into symphony in the form of vocal solos along with a singing chorus. After Beethoven came vinyl recordings and the combination of music and lyrics would be heard more often by the masses.[2]

Requisite in any form of Romance are some presence of the supernatural, an absence of central plot, a sense of adventure and a love affair. The Old English and Norse sagas extend themselves to a Romance of this particular kind. The magic of wizards, dragons, sorcerers, and giants permeates medieval English history and its oral tradition. Magic is valuable because it reinforces order where man's intellectual foresight wanes and it is a serious way of commanding success in worldly endeavours. Magic is an art.

Romantic music was also called art music, but Romantic is the term traditionally applied to the imaginative, passionate and predominant music of the nineteenth century. In addition to exquisite English poetry, this century saw the development and refinement of the English novel. The Philharmonic Society of 1813, the Crystal Palace of 1852 and the Royal Albert Hall of 1871 were England's new orchestra palaces and the arts flourished in England during this century just as they did elsewhere in Europe. Marches, church music, oratorios and choral music maintained popularity so most composers followed suit.

The guitar came into home music-making use in Europe after 1750 because it could be played either alone or as an accompaniment enjoyably. Around the end of the eighteenth century some musicians suddenly became free agents instead of being dependent on court royalty and churches for their patronage. Concert life as Great Britain knew it began developing about the same time as London's New Philharmonic Society was formed in 1852. In nineteenth-century England the music hall was new and the industrial folksong was developing into a popular music for city dwellers.

Blues, jazz, and Tin Pan Alley types of music were created in America in the early part of the twentieth century. Many black vocal groups were successful beginning in the 1940s, such as the Drifters and the Coasters and in America during the 1950s most songwriters created songs then sought these types of singers to sing them. Bill Haley recorded 'Rock this Joint' in 1952, 'Crazy Man Crazy' in 1953, and 'Rock Around The Clock' in April of 1954. Bill Haley and the Comets introduced the world to the fun of rock and roll music and Bill Haley was America's first rock star. In 1963 producer Phil Spector seized sound by engineering musicians thus creating his so called wall of sound. He combined classical rhythm sections consisting of violins and other stringed instruments. Two drum sets, four guitars, three basses contributed rhythm and blues sounds and created a very popular dance music. His songs were created for girl groups such as the Crystals and the Ronettes. These song lyrics were fun and trite, but most often repetitive.

The list of truly wonderful, Romantic female singers of the twentieth century is lengthy. Prolific songwriters and talented musicians made it possible for unique talents to shine through murky environments. Angelic presence, lyrics about infatuation and perfect voices were joined into rhythm and blues music by the girl groups. Special singing and songwriting talents were added to orchestrated music to lead these performers to sell records. Tina Turner fronted a rhythm and blues band in 1967 and became the world's most interesting rhythm and blues singer for the remainder of the millennium. Also, during the 1960s the contrived British pop group the Beatles showed up worldwide. To become famous was their goal and they became successful by having some talent, connecting with important people and continually playing music in Europe's many nightclubs.

Other young British musicians examined American blues through radio and records and fused together the two cultural experiences to form a new and much more inspirational rock and roll music. Music played by the American Negro in the nineteenth century was intrinsic to what became rock and roll music. This music evolved in the hands of guitar players and developed a life of its own.

The highly evolved English culture which created James Patrick Page will be described here by recalling a bit of English history, since his musical works are so obviously descendant from this England. Lord George Gordon Byron, born in London in January of 1788, took his seat in the House of Lords on 13th March, 1809. In the manner of an English gentleman he expressed emotion. It has been written in the Encyclopaedia Britannica of his many alleged love affairs, but thankfully for his readers, he wrote eloquent poetry. Well educated and up to the task, he chose the old Spenserian stanza form for his *Childe Harold's Pilgrimage* of 1812, 1816 and 1818 in which Lord Byron as

Childe Harold travels the earth experiencing unattainable love, sin, loss and the war field at Waterloo, France. Telling of Napoleon Bonaparte as hero, the clear beauty of Lake Geneva in Switzerland and the Bridge of Sighs at Venice, Byron gave a positive wealth of experience to his readers. The beauty and precision of this poet embodies the work of the Romantic poets.

In modern music Page created in the Romantic mode while he exhibited a strong classic blues background in his style. At times he writes lyrics about a sad love story such as 'Babe I'm Gonna Leave You'. Other works, like 'Ramble On' lay emphasis on strength of will being virtuous. Though hardly an excessive Romantic, he fell in love and was used by his girlfriend in his youth and this event hardened his will somewhat and led him to study alchemy, art, blues music, occult philosophy and the natural sciences. To mention the pastoral countryside of England, so beloved by Page, is to tell much about his life and work. He introduced the heavy metal movement with his music into the 1970s. This came after a decade of cultural revolts. These revolts were based on youth's crying out for civil rights and against the Viet Nam war. Important 1964 and 1965 statutes led to some progress with a drop in poverty for blacks and a change in white racial attitudes in the Southern United States. The Viet Nam war, however, dragged on for years until the greed of those involved was appeased.

The Romantic genre in music is deep, dark, meaningful and heavy. Also developing out of the Classical, precision and light are present in Romantic music, but these are always with less cultural emphasis and more elements of reality. Ignoring many small, man-made details, this music wants to make its audience feel, see and use.

During the nineteenth century opera performances in Britain contained lyrics. England's poetry gives the best feel for the Romance of this era and is well consummated by a glance at its most intensely Romantic poet: John Keats who was born on Halloween in 1795. His poetry mingled the senses and his two epic poems *Hyperion* and *The Fall of Hyperion* used the planet Saturn for their dark and heavy imagery. The two poems are concerned with the grand scheme of life and the latter continues the former, but reaches back to the beginning of *Hyperion* in an infinite circle. Old man Saturn comes to life in *Hyperion* in lines 135 to 137:

> This passion lifted him upon his feet,
> And made his hands to struggle in the air
> His Druid locks to shake and ooze with sweat[3]

This describes Jimmy Page on stage during the early 1970s when he manufactured a concert sound louder than an erupting volcano. In his three-hour sets were to be found audience-entrancing guitar solos on songs which quickly became rock classics such as 'Whole Lotta Love', twenty minute drum solos by John Bonham during 'Moby Dick', an erotic contortionist and soulful blues singer in the form of Robert Plant and the excellent, background musicianship of John Paul Jones.

The history of music in England is extremely irregular; it seems there was no flourishing domestic music, folk or otherwise in the one hundred year period of 1788 to 1888. This was the century in which English poets and novelists had developed their crafts to astonishing ripeness. Dramatic operas were the life support of publicly played music in England at this time. During this transitional period, music was not viewed as a serious and holy pastime, even though music had initially come from the Church and the British began to develop a preference for imported music. James Patrick Page and the other British guitarists who joined in the British invasion of America were not climbing into a prestigious profession, as electric guitarists in the 1950s, rather it was uncharted territory which they would chart. What Isaac Newton, Galileo, and Copernicus did for the solar system, what Locke, Smith and Veblen did for the age of reason and what Byron, Keats and Shelley did for English poetry, Jimmy Page did for twentieth century, Romantic, rock, guitar music; he defined it.

This book is an essay into a time when young musicians loved to create. I want to reminisce about a time, not so long ago, when rock stars packed seventy-five thousand people into arenas for three hours of distinctive and original music.

Winter

Beethoven's vision was for all men, and it was one of love.[1]
Francis Routh

The academic story of the beginning of the use of electronic music in London, England began in 1968 with the two musicians, Tristam Cary and Peter Zinovieff. The climax of their electronic music story occurred when they gave concerts to raise money to build a diversely, equipped studio. Zinovieff had developed his own electronic music system, Musys, in 1962.[2] Zinovieff and Cary enjoyed the broad range of expressions which electronic musical sounds extend to traditional instruments. The combination of electronic sounds and instrumental ones can be quite beautiful and when controlled by computers, the pitch, tuning, amplitude and sound simulations enable the orchestra conductor, in this case, Peter Townshend, to create and synchronise, store and save, interrupt and layer a unique sound.

In this and other ways the music of Peter Townshend in his rock band, the Who, approached the avant-garde. Although this music, in its earliest stages, seemed rudimentary, the compositional techniques were so simple and Townshend was so serious about his creative processes that his songs became consequential. Even though the music of the Who had a continuously onward development, its perpetual look forward into the future, its

18

uncichéd and stimulating sound did not approach the avant garde until their creation of the 1969 rock opera *Tommy*. The Led Zeppelin catalogue of music was too hedonistic and it relied too much on traditional blues motifs, to be considered avant garde. The Who's music filled a need for pleasure in sound and the group never strayed from rock music and escape is often suggested in the sound. Townshend embraced dissonance, distortion, and reverb with some accent on the thunder: the drums and bass. Their music does not communicate to each audience member: 'Oh, I can do that'. The music of *Tommy* is rife with contraptions and arrogant technique, yet somehow it is not alienating.

In the 1960s the Who did not contribute to the traditional fantasy that was being presented on television. The band made only rare appearances on television, the rest of their interviews were in person or on radio. The American teenage girl was being presented with clean and healthy male idols like Pat Boone, but Townshend was thin and pale and Roger Daltrey was a scruffy, street-fighting type who became a gutsy singer. The visual images which presented the band were quite unique: the serious, brooding Townshend, the non-stop clownship of Keith Moon, and the serious personality of John Entwistle made this band stand out beyond the other male rock symbols of the 1960s. While the individuals were never a part of the shallow and false sense of reality on television, the group lived and breathed in the real world and this life, they presented to us in music.

Peter Townshend really rocked, loud and clear, from the very beginning of his career. No blues here, just rebellious rock and roll which developed into his own avant garde rock opera stance. Pete Townshend defined rock and roll as much as anyone did, only without the borrowing from other musical genres. I find it remarkable that much of his music seems fresher than that of some new rock guitarists. I suppose the stellar nature comes from his honesty and integrity. He had help from Keith Moon, an extraordinary drummer with great rhythm who fell apart and died very young, but left a wonderful legacy nonetheless.

Townshend was one of the intellectuals of the 1960s guitarists, his music was not cerebral, but it always made a statement. If anyone was, Townshend was the original musical punk and his music claimed he could see for miles. Daltrey, Moon, Entwistle, and Townshend made great music together for fourteen years and were, without doubt, the most interesting band of the 1960s. Singer, Roger Daltrey, had a knack for sounding like a sinister street kid and a macho, sexy guy at the same time. He was very versatile and good at changing his singing style and the sound of his voice. 'I'm Free' and 'I Can't Explain' show him and the band singing together in a most wonderful harmony. Jimmy Page played guitar on the original, recorded studio version of 'I Can't Explain'.

I am perplexed that it took me so many years to really appreciate the Who's music. As I stand here listening to 'Who Are You', 'The Kids are Alright' and 'Substitute'. I realise how superior this band was in 1971. I loved their song 'Won't Get Fooled Again' at that time, but the synthesiser struck me with so much awe that it was difficult for me to associate the band with their other hit songs, the 1968 'Magic Bus' and the 1970 'See Me, Feel Me'. No one was ready for *Tommy*. Let's just say that Townshend wanted to get really good, and did. Each hit song, 'Pinball Wizard', 'I'm Free' and 'See Me, Feel Me' held lyrically profound insights into humanity and feelings coupled with music that made me tingle. Townshend sang to me when I was twelve: 'Don't cry, don't waste your time, it's only teenage wasteland' in 'Baba O'Riley'.

If you don't feel like getting emotional, and if you are ready to unwind at the end of a hard day, do not listen to music by the Who. Their music hits you up front in the face and forces you to think hard. Nobody else did that then. I always feel like Townshend took over where Jimi Hendrix left off, even though the two could not have been more different stylistically. Townshend was just as intense, serious about his art, gifted with talent and, thankfully, not as self-destructive. Hendrix was hot, but Pete Townshend was cool, really cool. The Who performed at the Monterey Pop Festival in 1967 and they followed Hendrix and his arson on stage, then Townshend pounded his guitar into the stage shredding it to bits. The Who loved to destroy their musical instruments after their performances. The difference between the two performers, however, was Hendrix wanted to make love to the world and Townshend was trying to explain the world. His music leaves its listener feeling clearer headed even though it glimpses that dark edge that is present in important rock music. The Who were rebellious without being repulsive on stage. Their music had none of the pounding repetition of hard rock even when Daltrey sang 'I can see for miles and miles, and miles and miles'. If there was an enlightenment in rock music, the Who were it.

Townshend's career holds many single song releases. He also played on Eric Clapton's Rainbow Concert in 1973, at Paul McCartney's charity and its resulting Kampuchea in 1981. Townshend's film *Quadrophenia* is about the 1960s mods being at war with the rockers and is worth appreciating if only for its historical value in documenting this most interesting period of the 1960s. *The Kids Are Alright* was one of the first 1970s rock documentaries and provides a glimpse of the Who and their unrehearsed antics. Townshend did a lot of things on stage to distract the audience from what he termed as his own lack of musicianship. His major talent was in writing lyrics and manipulating the Who's public image. The only member of the Led Zeppelin group who would aggressively construct a public image was Jimmy Page.

The Yardbirds were a group of young, serious musicians who worked very hard during the 1960s and made an eclectic type of music that was dependent on the blues. Eric Clapton, the first of three lead guitarists to front this band, began the improvisational, jamming style of guitar playing on stage. Later, Jeff Beck and Jimmy Page would add their own improvisational styles to this same band. Jimmy Page first worked professionally with Eric Clapton when Page produced the important John Mayall and the Bluesbreakers with Eric Clapton in 1966. The resulting singles were 'I'm Your Witchdoctor', 'Telephone Blues' and 'On Top of the World'. The Yardbirds' music was bluesy and simple, but when Page left the band dissolved within the decade in spite of surviving band members' efforts to continue. The double album *Shapes of Things* and the 1968 *Live Yardbirds!* featuring Jimmy Page are fair representatives of the music this band played.

When a male human being has a face which appears as half mischievous devil and half innocent and perfectly handsome schoolboy, a personality containing the endurance and spunk of an adolescent quarter horse, two parents who love him and he is witnessing the quagmire of London society at the age of thirteen, chances are he is about to go very far. James Patrick Page, born 9th January, 1944 in Heston, England began to play a Grazzioso brand acoustic guitar at twelve years of age. He grew up in Epsom and spent much time on a farm in Northampton, England. In the manner of an extremely determined English gentleman he decided to make his musical dreams come true. He delivered newspapers to get the money to purchase his first electric guitar.

His father, James Page, worked as a wages clerk for an aircraft works company and his mother, Patricia Elizabeth (Gaffikin) Page was a doctor's secretary[3]. Being an only child, Page knew at a young age his success in life would depend solely on his own ability. He listened to and learned to play all types of music, but was first influenced by Elvis Presley's rockabilly which Page could hear on the radio. Rock music had not yet defined itself in 1957, as Page was developing a knack for collecting and playing to obscure records by the American blues and rock musicians he came to prefer. The solitude of his childhood and a god given tenacity combined in this individual to form a very remarkable talent.

A type of psychological quirk is often set up in a child when he begins to enjoy solitude: the individual fiercely wants to do something better than anyone else, in whatever way possible, and thus ensure his own survival. Interestingly, only children rarely mind being alone, often though this environment creates a person who does not want to be merely accepted by society, he or she wants to reign over society. They develop cunning along with an inquisitive nature, become extremely astute at avoiding anything which would threaten their own survival, and develop a businesslike approach to work. In the case of Jimmy Page this approach consisted of playing guitar more than anyone else thus creating a flawless and important music.

Only children are very selfish and as adults we are unashamed of this virtue. We often limit our new experiences, we develop an overabundance of self-control and we refuse to be controlled or hurt by other people. Only children learn early to distinguish what kind of people cause pain and make early oaths to stay away from the type, as adults. People with no brothers or sisters, can be ruthless in severing relationships which are not

23

beneficial or have proven to be painful. We are very good at emphasising the positive and ignoring the negative aspects of reality. It is a simple matter of deciding what one desires to be real and concentrating exclusively on the positive. Anything negative is merely an illusion. Staying safe and inspired is all which is required to create the positive.

The apex of being an only child is that this privilege usually instils a drive to excel beyond the crowd. Attention to details and the painstaking efforts of perfectionism are pleasurable because of the knowledge that these are often overlooked by people who do not have the luxuries of time and solitude. The negative aspect of this luxurious childhood solitude is often the lack of development of an ability to forgive people their faults and shortcomings. It seems this inability to forgive stems from a lack of practice with siblings as a child. Only children truly believe they are special and this confidence leads many of us to great achievement. We expect of ourselves and, sometimes, too much of others which can lead to disillusionment when other people fail to live up to exacting standards. The danger is investing too much of one's energies at perfectionism in a career or at becoming wealthy and not directing efforts toward personal relationships. Though rarely cold or indifferent to their spouses, only children continue, as adults, to desire a great amount of support and praise.

Between the ages of twelve and thirteen people begin to think seriously about the world and feel the need to grow intellectually. This is the age when Jimmy Page chose his life's work. Learning alone and staying immersed in music, he took his guitar so seriously that three years later he was playing guitar publicly, first as a back-up guitarist for the beat poet Royston Ellis and at fifteen he played in a band called Red E Lewis and the Redcaps.

Many English boys of the 1950s played skiffle guitar and Jimmy Page was the most determined one of these to come out of England during my lifetime. Skiffle was based on American folk music of the 1920s and 1930s. The British invasion of America that ensued during the 1960s consisted of four major groups: the Beatles, the Rolling Stones, the Yardbirds and the Who cultivating their own unique tastes in music and playing their hearts out for years. Because of these and other bands such as the Searchers, the Hollies, Gerry and the Pacemakers, and the Kinks, the British suddenly had a music all of their own and the world joined them in enjoying this music.

Jimmy Page's notions of guitar playing were nurtured by his parents and he loved proving how responsible he could be by earning money by touring England's nightclubs with the band Neil Christian and the Crusaders in 1962, Carter Lewis and the Southerners in 1963, and the Mickey Finn in 1964. During this time Page also did a brief stint with a theatrical rock band led by an eccentric singer who could barely sing named David Sutch.[4] Screaming Lord Sutch and the Savages brought violent theatrics, stage makeup and spookiness to rock and roll in some of England's nightclubs in a very interesting way that would be copied later by Alice Cooper. Members of Lord Sutch and the Savages would all rise out of coffins before playing music and frequently Lord (David) Sutch would chop a piano to bits with an axe to conclude the show. David Sutch loved to entertain his audience and would employ actors in this staged show. One of the band's most famous skits involved a male dressed in a blond wig playing nineteenth-century, fictional character, Nellie Bly, getting murdered by Sutch. Band members wore spooky, white facepaint and black clothing while performing, long before it became fashionable for rock stars. Poor, practical Jimmy Page just wanted to make great music, consequently, he did not last long under the dictatorship of Lord Sutch. The savages also served as a training ground for future virtuoso guitarist, Ritchie Blackmore. Sutch drummer, Carlo Little, gave Keith Moon drumming lessons and Sutch taught Townshend theatrics.

Jimmy Page had heard popular music and blues music, but during his adolescence he came to prefer American rock music. At seventeen, after nightclub tours proved physically debilitating Page gave up touring to attend an art school in Sutton, England for eighteen months, where he studied fine art and painting. By 1965 he had begun his professional music career and he played guitar as a studio musician. He played back-up guitar for Marianne Faithful, Petula Clark, Brenda Lee, the Rolling Stones, on the Southerners' 'Your Momma's Out of Town' and he ended up on more than seventy-five per cent of the recordings to come out of England during the years of 1964 through 1967. Art to art. While attending art school he joined in local nightclub jam sessions and days were spent working in recording studios as a back-up session guitarist. He eventually learned to read sheet music and he crafted his future out of this early work.[5]

Establishment of an impressive track record came early for Jimmy Page. By 1967, he was a well-known London studio musician and had been seen in the film *Blow Up*. What separated him from the talented blues guitarists he had emulated earlier were his desires to create great music and to achieve. These hard-working years made him a professional guitarist who played powerfully and precisely. Jeff Beck, Jimmy Page and Eric Clapton were friends and they were the most promising of the Caucasian rhythm and blues guitarists to surface in England at this time. They played together for pleasure at home and Page eventually joined Jeff Beck to become a member of the Yardbirds, a band Eric Clapton had left far behind for a montage of talent called John Mayall and the Bluesbreakers.

When Jimmy Page joined the Yardbirds, he did so as a bass player, Jeff Beck played lead guitar. On Rock and Roll, the WGBH documentary, Page describes the harrowing adventures the Yardbirds experienced on their North American tours of 1966. It was when Jeff Beck failed to appear at a scheduled Yardbirds' set in San Francisco that Page began to be the band's lead guitarist. The Yardbirds toured America twice in 1966, and also Australia. Band members slept on buses and worked hard for little reward. The most important occurrence for Jimmy Page during his Yardbirds' membership was Peter Grant becoming the group's manager. Peter Grant managed a major portion of Page's career thereafter and to great success.[6]

Being thin and good looking, shrewd and cunning, charming and soft-spoken, aided Jimmy Page in the years that led him to become the letters patent of rock guitarists. Music of the 1960s slowly began developing into an inspirational and interesting medium. In 1961 stereophonic broadcasting began and then the FCC allowed FM stations this new technology. The blues path led right up to the door step of rock and roll music.

In April 1965 a music was made which later became an LP titled *Jimmy Page Special Early Works Featuring Sonny Boy Williamson*. The music of 'Don't Send Me No Flowers' is empty sounding and quiet spaces fill the rest of the five and a half minute song. Harmonica, vocals, organ and drums are detectable with a possible five plucked guitar notes. Jimmy Page is the only figure pictured on the album cover, but his sound on the recording is not as obvious. Listening to this LP is great fun anyway because it enables one to see what Page was doing at this time.

In 'I See a Man Downstairs' there is an audible bass line and it is great when the lead guitar pops in, however briefly.

Sonny Boy Williamson, whose real name was John Lee Williamson, began to record extensively in the 1930s, had a distinguished career as a blues singer and made a very influential harmonica sound. The original Sonny Boy Williamson died in 1948. The Sonny Boy Williamson on this recording is Sonny Boy (Rice Miller) Williamson No. II who often claimed to be the original. This Sonny Boy played with the Yardbirds at the Crawdaddy Club in England in 1963. Those old blues guys were an interesting bunch.[7]

The entire 1960s were full of enlightenment. There were many unique individuals around who made themselves heard. Brave, bold, spiritually and physically reckless poets of this decade made collective efforts to discuss, in an emotional context, what they saw as the superficial outlooks of older people. In 1964, the British invasion began in America which consisted of many singers, songwriters and musicians landing in the United States to entertain Americans. The Kinks, Gerry and the Pacemakers, the Who, the Beatles and the Rolling Stones were bands comprised of four and sometimes five members who entertained their audiences so as to sell records. The many American groups of Motown and the British groups dominated record sales during the last five years of this decade. The music of the Motown record company at this time was rather sweet and pretty so the British bands, with their rough edge, provided an interesting contrast.

For those who have said Page copied the music of his predecessors, the fact is Page worked and reworked songs by artists such as Little Richard before creating 'Whole Lotta Love' and 'Stairway to Heaven'. He listened to and played everything before he recorded with his own band. Concepts are similar in all art forms, but the music he has made is distinctly different from that of any other artists. He used many of the blues riffs he played in the Yardbirds on songs he created later. To list the major influences on Jimmy Page is easy and looks like this:[8]

Country, Rockabilly: James Burton, Johnny Meeks, Scotty Moore, Wes Montgomery;

Jazz: Kenny Burrell;

Rock and Soul: Little Richard, The Byrds, Chuck Berry Friends: Les Paul, Jeff Beck, Roy Harper;

Blues: Eric Clapton, Muddy Waters, Howlin Wolf, Buddy Guy, Willie Dixon, Robert Johnson, Freddie King, Otis Rush;

Acoustic: John Renbourne, Bert Jansch, Joni Mitchell, Manitas DePlata, Joan Baez.

The first recording of Jimmy Page occurred in January of 1963 from studio work which resulted in a hit song called 'Diamonds'. Two years later in February of 1965 Page released a solo single called 'She Just Satisfies'/'Keep Moving'. Elsewhere in England at this same juncture, John Bonham played drums for Terry Web and the Spiders and another band called A Way of Life. Robert Plant sang in the Crawling King Snakes. John Paul Jones did studio work in the same area as Page, in fact Jones arranged songs on The Yardbirds Little Games in 1966.[9] Cold and rainy, English weather gave British schoolboys plenty of time indoors. Playing music gave them something to do outside of school. Page had money enough for a house in Pangbourne before the formation of Led Zeppelin and he was always practical about money matters. Not so about his love, sexual and religious beliefs. Basically a shy adolescent, and certainly not promiscuous, he was too busy trying to earn a living to be scouting for sex. However, after his fame and fortune arrived hordes of females flung themselves at him,

29

but even still he was one of the more discriminating type of gentlemen and he has always liked young women. In his twenties he was never over-enthusiastic about having sexual adventures. His career was always a priority. His personality and character are marked by a sensitive emotional nature which he is particularly adroit at keeping hidden under a masterful and mentally tough exterior. He has never really been a seducer of women. He is and, as an adult, always has been opinionated about his music. His opinions are bold and he expresses them with conviction.

Since Jimmy Page was far too ambitious to have landed in factory work after secondary school, and there was no gap between his imagination and his cultural roots, he put more of the cultural wealth of England into his music than the British musicians who were his peers. His breadth of creative output is due to his willingness to take risks, do his homework and his courage. He gave up studio work when he had learned all he could from it and bravely formed a band. He dissolved that band, after the death of John Bonham, and he has stubbornly forged his own way since. He knows how to overcome obstacles through self-instruction. The intellect of Jimmy Page is both quick and deep.

The Yardbirds' song 'Heart Full of Soul', the Who's 'Can't Explain' and the Zombies' 'She's Not There' were not complicated or intricate masterpieces, but they were original and intuitive breakthroughs of creative effort. All of the 1960s and 1970s were phenomenal in that there were so many musicians who collectively contributed to a larger world outlook, one that seemed to want to create, explore and expand boundaries.

Like the Romantic and spooky story-teller extraordinaire, Edgar Allen Poe, who also explored the occult and the black hole of Satanism, Jimmy Page became strange for a time and fell down into that hole and hurt himself, but Page only self-destructed to an extent, then he recovered to resume his idealistic goals and visionary stance in the 1990s. Unlike Poe's nineteenth-century lyrics, the work of Page does not incorporate fear, haunting thoughts or nightmares. The imagination of Page does evade the material world, but he still purchased a house in Loch Ness, Scotland because of its reputation for being haunted and because it had been owned, formerly, by Aleister Crowley.

Of the mystery music created by Jimmy Page, the song 'Dazed and Confused' would be the most extreme example. Here the singer states: 'the soul of a woman was created below' and the bass guitar trudges slowly on behind Page's playing his electric guitar with a bow. The song gives its listeners an introduction to the darkness of Led Zeppelin music and Plant's curse upon his woman: 'Will your tongue wag so much when you end up in hell?', which is misogyny at its most representative point in history. This is as satanic as the music of Page ever became and elaborate technique would follow this 1969 effort.

Pressed for Time

I am certain of nothing but the holiness of the Heart's affections and the truth of the imagination.[1]

John Keats

In early 1968 James Page began experimenting musically with the three musicians for the band he desired. There were, then, a selection of guitar styles: jazz, flamenco, rock and blues and in his new band he turned up the volume just a bit more than the others and with both hands created one more: heavy-metal. Page heard the voice of Robert Plant in performance and was dazzled by it. Singer Robert Plant and drummer John Bonham were friends and had performed before audiences prior to Led Zeppelin. The most notable bands which Plant had fronted were the Band of Joy and Hobbstweedle. John Paul Jones and Page had been working in the same studio circles for years. John Baldwin took the stage name of John Paul Jones when he joined. There is a durability characteristic of Led Zeppelin music and this uniquely lasting quality derived from the band members' love of music.

These were exhilarating times for the four guys because they were passionate about what they were doing. Page and Jones were happy to be out of the drudgery of session work and the young bucks, Plant and Bonham, were innocently, anxiously and optimistically experimenting with the adventure of life by choosing to be travelling musicians.

After Page met with Plant and coaxed drummer John Bonham, with telegrams, into joining the New Yardbirds band, the four played their first gig together in Copenhagen on 7th September, 1968 and before the end of the year they had over one hundred performances under their belt.

At this time, Jimi Hendrix was playing his electric guitar music left-handed, and he similarly turned the guitar world upside down. He was a stellar talent who had toured America the hardest way imaginable, as a black person amid white prejudice. His greatness stemmed not only from his superior virtuosity and familiarity with his instrument, but also from an open nature which allowed him to be influenced by white blues musicians as well as by the traditional Mississippi Delta blues players. He became famous after he made his appearance at the 1967 Monterey Pop Festival in San Francisco, California. Jimi Hendrix is generally regarded as the greatest rock guitarist of all time.

Brilliant guitarists whom Page admired in the 1970s were Clarence White, Amos Garrett and Eliot Randall. During the 1970s the world would begin to see the electric guitar player quite frequently. Some could even make the guitar talk. The stories contained in the songs of most blues men were painful stories told in the only way they knew to express them. Blues music can make people happy and it often makes people feel sad, but great rhythm and blues music always makes people *feel*.

As early as 1972, Jimmy Page listened to a rhythm and blues guitarist named Buddy Guy, who was taught, personally, by Muddy Waters. By this time in American musical history music had become a huge business, one in which money was the qualitative factor, and Led Zeppelin was one of the biggest breadwinners in the industry. In Buddy Guy's book, *Damn Right I've Got The Blues* it is documented that members of Led Zeppelin frequented Buddy Guy's nightclub. These artists obviously knew to whom to listen. Just recently, I saw a video on MTV starring Jeff Beck and Buddy Guy playing a song called 'Mustang Sally' and for the first time I, personally, realised the allure of the music of Buddy Guy.

According to the 1997 January issue of *Smithsonian*, a medley of inventors are responsible for the modern electric guitar. Adolph Rickenbacker invented the electric guitar in 1931. Les Paul upgraded the guitar by turning the neck and the body into one solid piece in 1941. Leo Fender was close behind with his solid-body electric Broadcaster in 1948. Les Paul began to popularise the electric guitar sound in his public musical performances and in the 1950s he helped the Gibson guitar company, which was initially formed in 1902, with their design of the Les Paul Standard guitar line. Les Paul invented multi-track recording in the 1940s.[2]

No book about guitar players would be complete without mention of Django Reinhardt. Born of gypsies in Belgium, his style and guitar playing ability is still coveted in 1990s jazz circles. Though jazz music is not the music of pop culture, jazz music is popular and Reinhardt's jazzy, gypsy music attracts a cult following. He toured France as a member of a quintet and composed the extraordinary 'Bolero' and 'Montmartre' in the 1940s. Fast runs, original rhythmic structures and improvisations marked his performances. He expanded the sound of the acoustic guitar.

The Spanish and Romantic guitar player extraordinaire was Andres Segovia who brought his classical sound and the guitar into the limelight. The sound must be pulled out of a nylon-stringed acoustic guitar and Segovia did this with an inspiration of style. He started playing a Ramirez guitar then switched to a Hermann-Hauser. His guitar had an ebony fretboard with a body made of Brazilian rosewood. His timing and tonality were impeccable. In a 1977 interview with David Schulps of American rock magazine *Trouser Press*, Jimmy Page admitted to be one of a group of guitarists who loved Segovia's playing. Page loved to practise 'Rodrigo's Guitar Concerto'. In the same six hour interview he said he admired the style of guitarist Django Reinhardt.

By signing with Atlantic record executives Jerry Wexler and Ahmet Ertegun in 1968, Led Zeppelin insured their future financial success. At 1969 the music of Jimmy Page was being recorded with his Led Zeppelin band. *Led Zeppelin* was made rather quickly, in three weeks, and is enjoyable precisely because of its rough texture. This, their first album, is serious and contemplative. The first song lyrics begin with a look back at the days of youth even though the oldest member of the band at this time was twenty-five years of age. The songs exhibit tremendous feeling and the voice of Robert Plant is warm, unafraid and incredibly strong. His singing gives the feeling that everything can work out positively and that this world is a very special place. Two of these songs were written by Willie Dixon: 'You Shook Me' and 'I Can't Quit You Baby'. The brief 'Good Times, Bad Times' has a basic and simple beginning, the listener is keenly aware of the sound of each instrument, and the lead guitar is exceptionally quick and adept. 'Babe, I'm Gonna Leave You' has a beautiful beginning with a softly playing and interesting, acoustic guitar. It sounds like Spanish music and the listener is awed by the clarity of sound. 'You Shook Me' is messy and heavy with a harmonica and the guitar and vocal interplay which would become such an integral a part of a Led Zeppelin performance. In 'Dazed and Confused' there is a psychedelic sound, a slow and dramatic bass line with powerful and important drums. 'Your Time is Gonna Come' showcases the guitar and keyboards to interesting effect with the emphasis on the organ. 'Black Mountain Side' is completely instrumental and sounds bottomless.

There are extra drums played by Jasani. 'Communication Breakdown' has a searing electric guitar and 'How Many More Times' is psychedelic music at its best. This was quite a debut album; unpredictable and unlike anything the world had heard. It is fair to point out the two Willie Dixon songs because they are of the early American blues type of music which was suddenly beginning to be acknowledged and modernised by many British blues players, such as the Rolling Stones and Eric Clapton in the 1960s.

The onslaught of Led Zeppelin occurred so quickly that the band hardly had time to think about what was happening to them; they were rapidly becoming very well known as the 1970s began. The release of their first record was followed by tours of the United States and in the interim they released a second LP: *Led Zeppelin II*. 'Whole Lotta Love' sounds a screamer, at once frantic and out of breath, accompanied by cymbals and wonderful drum sounds. Five minutes and thirty three seconds in length, the song was obviously not designed for AM radio's three minute format, but FM stations found a way to fit this giant sound into their limited time frame because fans insisted on hearing Led Zeppelin music. 'What Is and What Should Never Be' contains vocal harmonies and this music pulls the listener through to the primordial world. My favourite feelings are derived from listening to the song 'Thank You'. On the twenty-three-year-old record of mine I experience all the peace of mind and affection of the companionship of a friend every time I listen. The keyboard playing of John Paul Jones completes the song here and to a greatly sublime effect. Their tours were what their fans lived for and Led Zeppelin delivered a lengthy and energetic performance. Their music was becoming.

After five years of exhaustive touring and much brilliant music making in 1973, the Led Zeppelin US tour broke the box office attendance records set by the Beatles. Led

Zeppelin eventually became the most popular rock band in the world. Jimmy Page and John Paul Jones made music by building on and extending previous musical genres, such as the Baroque. Musicians with such practical skill as Bonham, Jones and Page were rare in the rock music industry of the 1970s and the strong wail of Robert Plant was outstanding in its uniqueness. The conceptual dreams of the four musicians in this band constituted gorgeous music and a breathtakingly energetic stage performance.

The Beatles began the British invasion and Led Zeppelin finalised it, but America's musicians made their own significant contribution to the music scene of the 1960s. When I think of the 1960s I remember folk music, Sonny and Cher, and the rock poets Joan Baez and Joni Mitchell. Looking back through my record collection from the 1960s I find my favourite from Cream, where Jack Bruce sings most of the songs which are a hybrid of exploratory blues. Eric Clapton sings 'Outside Woman Blues'. On 'Strange Days' and 'Sunshine of Your Love' the two share vocal harmonies. Here there are spooky psychedelic tones that still sound interesting. Clapton was known as God around England at this time. Popular on the West Coast of the US from 1963 to 1967 was the suit music of the Wilson Brothers who combined vocal harmonies in the Beach Boys.

The most important poetic influence of the time was Bob Dylan. *Highway 61 Revisited* and *Blonde on Blonde*, two of his most notable recordings, contain the rock classics 'Like A Rolling Stone' and 'Rainy Day Women #12 & 35' respectively. His spontaneity and brilliant poetic mind created emotionally relevant lyrics which heralded the dawn of the Aquarian age.

Heavy metal harmony is complex, it is Gothic and natural and at this writing, it is old. The modes of heavy metal music are three of the seven medieval modes of music created during the Renaissance: the Aeolian, the Dorian and the Phrygian. The Aeolian mode consists of a triad of power chords on root, 7th, 6th, Am, G, and F respectively. Lydian and Mixolydian are modes often expressed in the music of Jimmy Page. There is little extremity and excess in the recorded electric guitar work of Jimmy Page. His stage performances were just the opposite, however, and audiences looked forward to three-hour performances consisting of loud, powerful music which simultaneously offered a peace of mind and a wistful looking forward.

I remember people accusing Led Zeppelin band members of being Satan worshipers. It seemed strange to me because of their musical sound being so positive and forthright. These accusations stemmed from a fondness Jimmy Page had for collecting Aleister Crowley memorabilia, which included the purchase of Crowley's haunted house in Scotland. Jimmy Page was uneducated, naive and wanted success badly enough to be intrigued by Aleister Crowley's simplistic books of magic. He also knew the rumours would add to his mystique and thus he manipulated the public, the press and all other people who were mystified by Aleister Crowley's spiritual investigations. Page served his apprenticeship in the teachings of Crowley by dabbling with morphine. Crowley had a reputation as a heroin addict before his death in 1947.

A group called Black Sabbath portrayed the Dark Age Droll Delirium to excess thus setting the occult trend in motion for a slew of future, heavy metal groups. Greed and idol worship are infectious and this dark trend caught on somewhat during the 1990s.

During the time I have been writing this book I have interviewed many male drummers and guitar players and countless female musicians. I know of many a male guitarist who legitimately and without reservation admires the work of Jimmy Page. There are a variety of books available about Led Zeppelin, some of which were written by the band's male acquaintances and others consist of great photographs of the quartet.

Much of the music of Led Zeppelin can be referred to as soul music because of the music's powerful emotional impact. Soul music is traditionally a racially divisive term which is only supposed to include music played by musicians with black skin, but I like to think as a civilisation we have progressed from this emblematic and problematic way of thinking. Traditional soul greats are James Brown and Otis Redding, whose 'Sitting on the Dock of The Bay' had a mass appeal. Since most soul artists began singing gospel music in church they came to call theirs a soul music. The soul music genre is huge and should include some Led Zeppelin music, but should not include formulaically written songs. Fans of soul music describe the music as deep, thrilling and yet significant in an enduring fashion.

Amber in Starlight

*Music should strike fire from the heart of man and bring
tears to the eyes of woman.*[1]

Ludwig Van Beethoven

On The Road, the most influential work of writer Jack
Kerouac, hit bookshelves in 1957. The reading of it gave
way to a mild revolt by some white, American, middle-
class youth. Known as beatniks, their inclination consisted
of an effort to cast off materialistic ties such as houses, jobs
and cars, which were symbols of security to their parents. It
is also possible to consider T S Eliot's much earlier epic
poem *The Waste Land* as a promoting factor in many young
college student's desires to cast off constricting social
mores. In the 1960s, it was a general dissatisfaction with the
status quo which led some poets, drug addicts, musicians
and sometime political activists, who were irrational in
their behaviour to live by the ideals that life should be for
self-realisation, self-actualisation, fun, poetry, sex and love
and not simply for making money. They hoped for life to
be a transcendent experience, not a job. This group made
way for the hippies whose psychedelic music of the mid
1960s was part of the Romantic genre of music because of
its intense emphasis on exploration and cultivated use of
the human imagination. Available in book form in 1956,
was *The Doors of Perception* by Aldous Huxley in which the
reader is told how ingesting mescaline is helpful in

achieving a state of egolessness and in being able to see how all people are one, all is all and all is each. An individual attains this type of consciousness with ingestion of mescaline because it lowers the amount of glucose which normally goes to the brain.

The first impression I have of what I call rock and roll music came to me in early 1968. On this day my babysitter, Ann, was very excited about taking me to the Ice Palace to see Jim Morrison and his group, the Doors, whom Morrison named after Huxley's book. Jim Morrison is alleged to have been the type of person who had a will of iron which no human could stand in the way of. One of the descriptions the folklore written about him offers is him as most persistently enjoying experiments with his own bio-chemistry by using psychedelic drugs, alcohol and even mescaline from the peyote cactus. Ann and I did not know all this about Morrison in early 1968 preceding what was to be a very important and monumental event of seeing him and his band at the Ice Palace. Apparently he got into some trouble in Florida and was apprehended for taking his clothes off in front of an audience so we were prevented from seeing the handsome Jim Morrison in concert. That day, before we learned we would be unable to see Ann's favourite human being, our listening consisted of music played by groups such as Iron Butterfly, Tommy James and the Shondells and the Yardbirds. 'Inna Gadda da Vida', 'Crimson and Clover' and 'For Your Love' were the respective hit songs. I had, by this stage of my life developed my own taste in music which included anything to which I could dance. Iron Butterfly's 'Inna Gadda Da Vida' was a little too deep for me at first, but eighteen-year-old Ann seemed so beautiful and chic that I gradually developed a taste for a particular type of heavy-metal music. By the time we returned home that night, Ann had purchased the Doors' 'Light My Fire' and the two of us

41

chose to partake in a marathon of music played by the Doors before we slept. From that day forward Jim Morrison became a hero of mine and that night when I dreamt of him he wore a light, blue shirt and appeared to me as a deeply intelligent, strong and warm human being. This is the image I have retained of him throughout my life. Morrison was the most famous poetic advocate of the beatnik belief, but he became most notorious for his sexual persona and passionate singing. I felt quite important in 1970, when The Doors titled their album *13*, because I turned thirteen that year. Shortly after this adventure Jim Morrison died, at the age of twenty-seven, of heart failure, in a bathtub in Paris, France. I came down with mononucleosis and took to my bed watching Dark Shadows at 12.30 p.m. every day and developed a fondness for wearing dark eye make-up. Since this time I have not had a hero, but I value music which is, at the least mysterious and creepy and at its best, obtuse and Romantic. I have missed Jim Morrison with an extreme passion all through my life.

When I turned sixteen in 1973, maintaining popularity and becoming widely read in America were the Romantic fantasy adventure novels of J R R Tolkien who died that same year. British born and a professor at Oxford, his 1937 book *The Hobbit* tells a story of a chubby and peace-loving people who live in Middle Earth. His later works *The Fellowship of the Ring*, *The Two Towers* and *The Return of the King* are more developed stories about his darling hobbits, were published in England in 1955 and were most certainly read by Led Zeppelin members James Patrick Page and Robert Plant. The writings of J R R Tolkien are mildly detectable in the lyrics of 'Ramble On', from *Led Zeppelin II*: 'In the darkest depths of Mordor, I met a girl so fair / but galem, the evil one crept up and slipped away with her'.

In Tolkien's *The Fellowship of the Ring* Mordor is the place where the shadows lie in the little poem which prefaces his story. Gollum is a scary, little creature described on page twenty-one of the 1985 edition. Other elements, such as wringwraith in the song 'The Battle of Evermore', from Tolkien's novel *The Lord of the Rings* would show up in the work of Led Zeppelin from time to time.

In 1970 came *Led Zeppelin III* in which Bonham, Jones, Page and Plant give in to the blues with 'Since I've Been Loving You' a mighty contribution to the genre. Truly the stellar tune of side one, the song is over seven minutes of the night-time type of love. 'Gallows Pole' is a folk song that had been passed down through the oral, blues tradition and the song is given great intensity by Robert Plant who screams at the top of his lungs and by Jimmy Page who plays the banjo as if he had played it all of his life. Interestingly enough, this marked the first time he had ever played the banjo. The music of 'Tangerine' tends toward the psychedelic and is the last of their introspective creations before the music of Led Zeppelin came to reflect a broader and more universal tone. Nevertheless the sounds on this recording would come to be definitive of the heavy metal sound. 'Tangerine' is Robert Plant emoting through the lyrics of Jimmy Page. A song like 'Tangerine' shows its writer, Jimmy Page, to be an individual who is feeling a bit uncomfortable in his present incarnation. He plays a pedal steel guitar on 'Tangerine'. The two most notable features of *Led Zeppelin III*'s 'Immigrant Song' are the consistent precision of the drums and the simplicity of the guitar work. The song consists of few variations, actually it is simply the chords A and E then A to F#m, B to C and much expertly executed bass music ends the song. In its utter simplicity it glimpses the profound. On the B side of this single was a seldom heard gem called 'Hey, Hey What Can I Do?' which has hilarious lyrics. The songs on this LP differ greatly from one another. 'Out on the Tiles' is a bit more complicated musically, but the wonderful drums are right there, with no special effects and Robert Plant is doing what he does best which is talking about love. 'Gallows Pole' is a song I love and this is why: for half of the song the guitar entirely replicates a drum beat perfectly, and I do mean perfectly, and I am unable to listen to the song without dancing. Interesting lyrics, folk sounds, psychedelia, blues, loud and powerful music. What a sense of accomplishment its creators must have felt.

Led Zeppelin III is straightforward, powerful and majestic. On the inner spirals of my vinyl record is inscribed *Do What Thou Wilt*. 'Immigrant Song' begins the album and contains images of the midnight sun and Valhalla. Ships are headed for a western shore. In these songs it is obvious Led Zeppelin has developed their own significant sound. 'Bron-yr-Aur Stomp' is a song named after the cottage in Southern Wales where the band members stayed with their families during the creation of this music. 'Hats Off to (Roy) Harper' is a strange and squeaky salutation to the British folk singer Roy Harper. There is an entire world in the library of Led Zeppelin music, it is one of history, love and beauty. I would like to take this opportunity to thank them for colouring the 1970s with their exceptional music.

Robert Plant held a studied interest in the Celtic soldiers and heroes of the past and Jimmy Page studied anything which would lend mystery and mystique to his persona. At this time Led Zeppelin music and lyrics were simple and soulful; however, their music never became predictable and did not resemble any other. They remained close to the earth which led to their creation of the song 'Stairway to Heaven'. Their offstage behaviour is said to have obliterated western canons of taste, but on stage they were hard-working, hard rock musicians. Having what it takes to make great music is esoteric and there is more to musical talent than practice. A musical talent of the Led Zeppelin type is innate and truly gifted musicians naturally gravitate toward their specific instruments at a young age.

Led Zeppelin live shows were arenas for creative improvisation in their music and they played longer than most bands did at that time. Their shows were not the tremendous theatrical exhibits which were becoming prevalent. The music is what mattered to Led Zeppelin.

Music at this time became a very valuable commodity, a huge money making business, consequently it began to be approached as a business by record makers and also by many people who wanted to be successful in the music business. The artists of Led Zeppelin stayed steadfastly creative where many other bands used formulas which were devised to sell records.

The innocence of the 1960s had disappeared and was not selling anymore. Music of groups like Peter and Gordon and the Beatles had to either toughen up, change and expand or fade away. The light and trite pop song was not totally passé by 1970, but there was a newer market. There was a harder, streetwise and tougher language becoming popular because it was a more accurate reflection of the world and this hipper talk sold records. Late mannerism and Rimbaud met music. A number of musical groups came in to view in full bloom with this raucous lyrical style of song. Led Zeppelin's lyrics were reflective of this style, but still retained a softness while their music was much harder and louder than that of any other rock band.

Led Zeppelin music always had a texture not limited to guitar sounds which was due in part to the keyboards of John Paul Jones. These musicians displayed themselves as big-hearted human beings. Robert Plant has a big, grisly, masculine voice. John Bonham was big and strong and made a very hard, loud and big drum sound and Jimmy Page played a quite voluminous and heavy guitar sound.

Led Zeppelin music was appealing to people who required more than yea, yea, yea from a song lyric. Everything was bigger in the 1970s: fashion, air pollution and artists and their income. Suddenly there were no rules to music making and by 1978 there were plenty of scary bands around of which I was afraid. Some breathed fire and wore bloody clothes, but Led Zeppelin just rocked away the decade.

Increased cash flow never contaminated the music of this band, in fact, 'Whole Lotta Love' came from their second album and was their biggest seller, but this song was nothing compared to what they came up with later. They were self-destructive, beautiful, unbelievably robust, yet humanly frail, original and profound; John Bonham, John Paul Jones, Jimmy Page and Robert Plant were rock music's Romantic villains in the 1970s.

As early as 26th December, 1968 Led Zeppelin toured the United States. Their first United States tour began in Denver, Colorado. Four days later they appeared in the auditorium of the Catholic University called Gonzaga in Spokane, Washington. April of 1969 found them at a Los Angeles arena, October took them to Michigan, Illinois, Ohio, Boston, Massachusetts and Syracuse and Buffalo, New York. Still touring behind their second album in February of 1970, they appeared in Denmark, Sweden, Finland and the Netherlands.

As a twelve-year-old girl sitting in the passenger seat of a Buick Riviera and driving east on Sahara Avenue in Las Vegas, Nevada, I saw a billboard on the corner of Maryland Parkway and Sahara which bore the words Led Zeppelin. Their Las Vegas Convention Center appearance was to be 4th April, 1970, the last date of their North American tour which they cancelled.

Where mid-century music was either a record listening at home, ballroom, or night club type of experience, after

Elvis Presley and the Beatles appeared, Jimi Hendrix performed at Monterey in 1967 and the famous three day, psychedelic, hippy, rock festival in Woodstock, New York in 1969, the way was paved for the huge arena, stadium and outdoor festivals attended by thousands in the 1970s. One of the favourite methods of hippy revolution would come to be attendance of loud rock concerts. This loud rock phenomenon began in the late 1960s and its potential became multiplicative. This decade was socially reformative. By 1970 many a rock song contained a political message. Love, peace and liberty were fashionable in music. What made Led Zeppelin music so unique and immediately popular, was the lyrical emphasis on pleasure and lust without mention of wars or civic problems.

The influence Jimi Hendrix had on rock and roll music outlasted the few short years of his recordings (1966 to 1970). His music was strange and I delegate him as the creator of psychedelic music. Not only did he play rapid chord progressions in a blues style, but he had an additional layer of sound in his music, which can only be called psychedelic. His playing was sloppy, all over the place and as brilliant as fire.

This somewhat popular sound of the 1960s was associated with the hallucinogenic drug called LSD or acid. Psychedelic rock, also called acid rock, was primarily a cult type of music. One of the successful acid rock groups was Jefferson Airplane who, later became known as Jefferson Starship. They invented the light show which visually accompanied their musical performance. This sound has been identified as originating geographically in the region of San Francisco. Psychedelic rock faded out rather quickly and was replaced by its antithesis, disco, in the mid 1970s. Disco was a dance sound specifically designed for record playing in public dance clubs which were called discotheques. This sound was modulated at one monotonous tempo and usually the droning sounds came from synthesisers. The psychedelic beat advocates wanted a transformation of social mores. These gentlefolk were followed by the discotheque devotees who were people who could not get enough of material gratification. Cocaine was the drug of choice for the discotheque people and effects of the drug enabled them to hop from club until the sun came up in the morning. The disco craze did as much to instil a materialism into the American culture as did the later continuum of Republican presidencies of 1980 until 1992.

Jimmy Page was unlike his young contemporaries in his approach to musicianship. Most fame seekers of this era were simple and sloppy in comparison since they obviously felt technical knowledge would stifle their creativity or take away the blues of their sound. The precision and constant exploration and experimentation made the difference in his music. It is knowing the rules that allows one to break them.

The questing for a dream is very Romantic and questing is what Page and Plant were doing in the 1970s. The fourth Led Zeppelin album was recorded in 1970 and released in November of 1971. This is the one of which they would be proudest and live to love. The album cover's art work portrays a desirable and simple ecological balance: an old man is shown in harmony with nature in spite of the grey, air pollution and urbanisation shown behind him. This would be the way Henry David Thoreau looked while building his cabin at Walden. This band would be one of the first to design all their own album jackets. The album was known by a number of names, but was never given a title.

Historically, bohemians were a love group of struggling artists in Paris around 1900. From 1966 until 1976, America was full of a similar group called hippies. These individuals were around fifteen to thirty years of age and some of them made a collective effort to rebel by de-emphasising middle-class values, sometimes protesting in the streets, listening to rock music and loving each other. In 1971 Led Zeppelin's fourth album gave many people of this inclination a song they could relate to: 'Stairway to Heaven'. The song's lyrics are printed on the inner sleeve and therein a spiritual optimism about the future. Somehow this song helped to perceptually overcome what was seen as an overly oppressive society and the song makes the listener feel as though the world could be a better place through universal love. The massive overdubs on 'Stairway to Heaven' were installed at Island Records.

There is also a lot of sex appeal in this music. 'Black Dog' is all about watching honey drip a flaming heart. Here is a very unique type of music; even twenty years later there is something extremely interesting about a Jimmy Page guitar lick. There is no restraint in 'Rock and Roll' and the song takes the listener into an overly energetic realm. To see Jimmy Page unleashed onto the stage playing the song fulfils every earthly, female desire. 'The Battle of Evermore' would later become a classic as would most of the songs off of this recording. It is to 'The Battle of Evermore' that I make the connection to the work of Beethoven. If his 'Pathetique' had lyrics they would be similar to these. 'Stairway to Heaven' is Robert Plant wondering, being prolific, and telling us how everything still turns to gold. It has been the most requested song in the history of radio. 'Misty Mountain Hop' takes its title from a place in J R R Tolkien's *The Hobbit* and consists of intense vocals, hard, hard drums and Robert Plant insisting that he really does not know. 'Going to California' still takes me to an imaginary place even if it is not in the United States. The song is peaceful, acoustic and sublime. This album defined the band. On 23rd February, 1972, the band performed publicly in San Diego, California and in June, Houston, Texas. July took them to Kansas, Missouri, Louisiana, Florida, Kentucky and North Carolina.

Houses of the Holy followed. The artwork on this album cover is of quite beautiful, naked and blonde children scaling a stone mountainside. The colours of the picture on the inside bear a psychedelic hue on a mountain top with a man holding a woman up to the sky. The moon peeps over a castle top in front of the pair. The music here is the band's most heart-warming and beautiful. With song titles of 'Dancing Days' and 'The Ocean' this music can only be called transcendental. Much of the music here is acoustic and soft, refined and truly incredible. The beginning cut 'The Song Remains the Same' is a hopeful ten lines. The image perceived by me of this music, in 1973, the time when I first became aware of Led Zeppelin was: to be wise is to be Jimmy Page and to be detached from everything except for good fortune is to be Robert Plant. Page is exquisite here in his sensitive playing and in 'Over the Hills and Far Away' he seems to be in love.

There was no existing rock aesthetic at this juncture and Led Zeppelin defied their reputation by transcending the electric blues standard they created on their first two albums.

Thunderous Strength in Stargroves and Stadiums

And Morning from Her Orient Chamber Came[1]

John Keats

Count Von Ferdinand Zeppelin built an airship in 1900 and he gave it his surname. From 1907 until the end of World War I, the Zeppelin (LZ-1) airship was used in war. In 1910, Deutschland inaugurated commercial passenger service in Zeppelins. After a four day journey across the Atlantic Ocean, less than a mile above the ground, attempting a landing in May of 1937, Zeppelin's Hindenburg exploded in hydrogen fire. There were sixty-two survivors.[2] The burning image appears on the first album cover produced by Led Zeppelin. The Treaty of Versailles of 1919 prevented new manufacturing of the Zeppelin. In 1944, the year of Page's birth, the German Zeppelin company factory was bombed and destroyed. The wealth accumulated by the Zeppelin family most probably factored into Page's usage of the name for his band, although the initial idea is said to have come from the talented drummer from the Who, Keith Moon.

Large areas of the city of London, England were destroyed in World War II. After a three year lull, many air raids resumed in London in June of 1944 and continued well into 1945. The atmosphere was filled with loud, frightening noise.[3] Hard times are the best words to describe the economic climate for the middle class of England in the early twentieth century, but the British are not an average people. Although the Germans are supposed to be exemplary for their work ethic, it seems their motivation for work differs from the English drive. The British work because they know it is the proper thing to do.[4]

Unlike American youth, the masses of British working-class youths are not herded into higher schools of learning such as universities. Instead they learn early to be industrious. It is obvious to them in their teens that they will have to do something. Humility runs rampant in the typical British personality no matter what level of success they sometimes achieve. They are taught to memorise poetry in grade school. I attended private, American Catholic schools and I never had to memorise a word until college.

Born in Heston, Middlesex, England,[5] Jimmy Page was involved in the sport of soccer until music caught his interest. Surrey schoolboys in Great Britain were encouraged in their soccer matches, but the parents of Page encouraged their son's musical obsession. Page bought instructional manuals, listened to records and forever after played his guitars. The adolescent part of his youth was spent in Feltham, a noisy community in close proximity to Heathrow airport. In 1952, the smog of London was so toxic that it killed four thousand people in the space of four days. The options for employment in 1967, according to *The Times* of London, were as follows: Senior Library Assistant at University of Essex and Professor of History at University of New England. To be a Technical Editor for *Farmer and Stock Breeder* required this: 'The man we want will probably be in his thirties, technically well qualified (BS or NDA) and a pace ahead of current thought and practice, a lucid writer'. Also advertised were available positions for training officers and executive assistants.[6] Page had already developed his own unique and marketable skills, quite similar to those desired in the advertisement. By this time he had been hired by Brian Jones to play guitars for the film soundtrack *A Degree of Murder* in 1964 and had become house producer for Andrew Loog Oldham's, new label called Immediate Records. Besides being extremely personable, charming and friendly he knew how to network.

The cutest thing I have ever seen in my entire life is Jimmy Page in a clip of a 1958 television programme, The Huw Wheldon Show in which Page and another young fellow play skiffle guitar and sing a song called 'Mama Don't Wanna Play No Skiffle No More'. He tells the host of the programme he is going on to a career as a biological researcher. I suppose you could say Page has mastered life affirming life processes since he has outlived many a performer who was his contemporary.

Led Zeppelin began touring America in late 1968, playing 'Whole Lotta Love' and 'Dazed and Confused' and fulfilling old Yardbirds tour obligations. In the WGBH documentary *Rock and Roll*, Page tells how he developed a bag of guitar tricks in the Yardbirds and was eager to pull them out and use them in his new band Led Zeppelin.[7] I describe the music he played at this juncture as deep blues.

The music and lyrics of all heavy metal bands are based on a carpe diem philosophy. This philosophy stems directly from the English Renaissance poetry written by Robert Herrick, Andrew Marvell, and John Donne. To Page, however, the immortality of the lyric was secondary to the immortality of the music. Page thought he could fly over the world and enable others to transcend the boundaries of worldly life through sound and this overcoming is thought by him to be tied to the balance and love between a man and a woman. In the 1960s he had a girlfriend whose name was Lynn Collins.

The adventures he experienced on the road during his musical tours became hazardous to his health and it is a wonderful miracle that he lived through and beyond them. As stated earlier other stars of the 1970s were not so fortunate. 1976 saw Led Zeppelin earning over one million dollars for their New York Madison Square Garden shows. However, the movie *The Song Remains the Same* shows two hundred thousand dollars of this missing from a hotel safety deposit box. They were Atlantic record's biggest moneymaking act. In 1977 Led Zeppelin cancelled ten concert dates because of the sudden death of Karac, the beloved five-year-old son of Robert Plant. The band ceased performing live for two years.

The album artwork on *Led Zeppelin II* is as dark and dreary as that on their first. The black and white photograph on the cover displays ten people, four of which are band members, dressed in the Nazi storm-trooping style. The little colour which appears is a faint, purple gleam which appears as an aura around the head of Jimmy Page and in the yellow clouds over the Zeppelin behind them. The interior artwork reveals the band's desire to be world famous. The biggest hit song from this record, 'Whole Lotta Love' was borrowed from Willie Dixon's 'You Need Love'. 'What is and What Should Never Be' provides a glance at where the band is headed musically with its interestingly unique rhythms and its thirteenth chord. Robert Johnson had his own version of 'The Lemon Song' before that of Jimmy Page.

'Thank You' denotes love and nothing but wonderful sounds emanate from the keyboards. 'Heartbreaker' sounds like wartime and Plant bemoans the way his woman converses during their intimate moments. In 'Living Loving Maid' Plant has taken notice of his female neighbour's alimony payments, but everything eventually meets his approval because, as he says: 'she's just a woman'. 'Ramble On' is a soulful rocker with an acoustic beginning and connotes a beginning to the band's world adventures. I have decided 'Moby Dick' can only be truly appreciated by drummers or men. 'Bring It On Home' brings their second effort to a boring close.

Page never became disenchanted with his music production, until the death of John Bonham, after which it took close to a year before he played his guitar. Page never created solely to sell. His music does not tend toward the monotonous with repetitive performances because he makes efforts to improvise his performances each night and his music is intricate, farsighted and pleasing to hear. The fourth and fifth albums are gifts which contain more pleasant melodies, but still make great strides in scale, rhythm and tempo variations. There are few detectable repetitive patterns even though the rhythm is there. His music emphasises precision, restraint and exactness from the fourth album on. Harmonies are more expressive of emotion and subjective feelings which clearly classifies his music as of the Romantic genre, but of course with the flexibility of his created mode.

The overladen orchestration which Page has developed and refined is consistent with the Neo-Romantic period in which Richard Strauss created in the early part of the twentieth century. The mystic bent of Jimmy Page found a perfect arena for expression in this format. An emphasis on beauty and sensitive emotions are what keep his music afloat in a calculated musical atmosphere. The importance of art is determined by the amount of money it generates and sometimes by the honesty, beauty and integrity of the work. In this chapter is a description of intensity apparent in the work of these artists. Quality of music by my friends was judged by the loudness of the sound of the power chord and the degree of good looks possessed by the lead singer. Quality of music in the late 1970s would be defined by record sales, and the definitions of quality would not be the same as in the 1870s by churches, courts and wealthy connoisseurs.

Dramatic stage effects and white doves were added to the shows given by Jimmy Page on his ninth American tour with the rock band Led Zeppelin. Page had slipped into the guitar playing role fifteen years earlier, reproduced all the great music he could in studios, so by the time he was famous he could create any kind of music he damn well pleased and it would be an other worldly and fascinating flourish. He must have listened, if only slightly, to the irritating reviews given to *Houses of the Holy* because its following recording, *Physical Graffiti*, turned out to be the hardest rocking album of Led Zeppelin's entire career. People were confused, perhaps some were disappointed that *Houses of the Holy* had such an acoustic feel and was not the blistering heavy metal which the band delivered so seductively in their three hour concerts. The band implemented video screens, on the tour of 1975, so fans far away could get a better view of them.[8]

Heavy metal music was a new art form, created by Led Zeppelin between the years of 1969 and 1974, by which time Page and his bandmates were being transported from show to show in their own chartered aeroplane which they called the *Starship*. *Houses of the Holy* and intermittent slices of *Physical Graffiti* were being recorded at the mobile recording studios which belonged to Mick Jagger, another famous rock star. These recording facilities were often parked outside his manor called Stargroves. Jagger paid twenty-five thousand pounds for this sixteenth century mansion, near Newbury, England and he later sold the same property for two hundred thousand pounds. That stint Jagger did at the London School of Economics must have taught him a thing or two about real estate investment. Jimmy Page managed his money by refusing to spend any of it foolishly and friends came to call him lead wallet.[9, 10]

The year 1974 also saw the band mastering an LP on their own record label of Swan Song at numerous recording locations, one of which was called Headley Grange. When released the double album called *Physical Graffiti* received rave reviews, reached number one in Billboard, and sold for $11.98. These lush orchestrations set the mood for a travelogue in music. A trip to a far away place that holds mystery, adventure and romance for all.

After much world travel and success Led Zeppelin had released five recordings and they began to exhibit a confidence in their music which enabled them to boldly experiment with their sound and by being daring they extended their genre widely. *Physical Graffiti*, their sixth album, is a new musical sound. They began work on this double album in 1973 and the final product contains the epic 'Kashmir'. This recording is extremely interesting and defies categorisation, the songs are as different from each other as they are from anything else they had recorded previously.

Before I knew the song 'Kashmir' to be about Plant's drive through Kashmir and all of the other Moroccan influences, I thought it was simply the best example of a rock singer and, absolutely, the most feeling ever put into a drum beat that I would ever hear. When I first heard this song in 1977, I came to consider Jimmy Page as the most intelligent band leader in the world. After they storm-trooped the United States in their ninth American tour and they hauled hundreds of thousands of dollars worth of equipment, musical and otherwise, to more than thirty-three cities, these British superstars graced Great Britain with five shows at London's Earl's Court Arena on 17th, 18th, 23rd, 24th and 25th May, 1975.[11]

Physical Graffiti is the most brilliant collection of songs produced during the 1970s. It is not the arrogant lyrics or title of 'In the Light' that make me say this. It is the delicate feelings Page delivers through his plucked guitar notes and the wide array of musical expressions present on this dual album. Page nearly always says he is nobody in interviews and he often adds that there are many guitarists who he considers better than himself. He seems to credit much of success to the fact that there were simply not that many guitar players around London during the 1960s. This shows a great deal of intelligence on his part and this attitude is not mere pretension. His personality is dualistic in the sense that he is humble much of the time, but is capable of being most arrogant. I do know that when I hear 'Bron-yr-Aur', his two minute, acoustic instrumental between 'In the Light' and 'Down By the Seaside', I feel as if this world might be a safe place to have children in after all.

In the lyrics of 'In the Light' Robert Plant sings: 'you will find the road'. This is as didactic as rock music gets and this particular song could easily be an outline for a rock opera. This album relates the band's wealth of experience to their listening public. My favourite cut off *Physical Graffiti* is 'Trampled Under Foot' which features Jimmy Page's backwards echo and his use of the wah-wah pedal, Plant is macho while he is talking about love, the organ and keyboards of John Paul Jones are prominent, John Bonham plays his fabulous, behind the beat, soulful style, and Jimmy Page displays fast, tricky, super cool guitar licks. The band is precious here, truly a gift from God. Next, 'Kashmir' is eerie and promises to mean something important. Stellar here, as far as exemplary of their musical development goes, is 'Ten Years Gone' combining the acoustic with the intricate electric guitar sounds Page is capable of and the beginning of his layering on of guitars techniques is most evident in this song. The song is Plant's vocals surrounded with what must be the most interesting sampling of different guitar styles in one song.

I have already explained how Page arrived at this level of artistry; by demanding a certain high level of expertise from himself and only from himself. His fellow musicians could not have failed to deliver brilliance as well as a result of being in his company day after day. Page and Plant had explored Morocco and its music and culture and this experience created an authentic atmosphere in 'Kashmir'. The song begins with a dramatic tone and a lyrical reference to the sun. As Plant dreams, and travels lyrically through the song, the music is slow and deliberating. Gradually, as the music becomes louder, he sounds more and more fearful. The tone here is deep and heavy. The vocals are serious and dramatic and the music throughout follows suit. References are to a wasted land and a search for feelings. Plant never surpassed the importance of his vocals on this song. 'Kashmir' captures much of his masculine strength and the music paints a dismal picture. Beginning at the time of this release, Led Zeppelin music fixed the standard of metal music for the remainder of the 1970s. They were in the media much of the time and this is most assuredly because they toured so much and improved upon and dramatised music at this time. The crux of what Page had instilled into a musical phenomenon is here: blues, albeit stretched to its breaking point, heavy metal at its best in 'Trampled Underfoot' and the folksy camaraderie in 'Boogie with Stu'.

'Custard Pie' is detestable no matter what its genre. 'Sick Again' is a terrible sounding miscellaneous and the lyrics are even worse. 'The Rover' is Plant attempting, lyrically, to expand his audience's social skills by intermittently screaming: 'if we could just join hands'. Thankfully, Page interrupts boldly and his brilliant, overplaying guitar redeems the song. The most rigid, but possibly the finest guitar licks on the record are to be found on 'In My Time of Dying', but then the annoying vocals of Plant surface to ruin the song. Vocals by Robert Plant were always either completely brilliant or extremely irritating. He does not give enough to the substantial lyric here to make it seem like he cares, so why should we?

As most of these songs glimpse the best that rock music could deliver 'The Wanton Song' is an example of what went wrong in many studios during the 1970s. At this time many artistic musician types thought they could produce epic art on vinyl. Subsequently, they found mellotrons, synthesisers and theremins and proceeded to make as many strange sounds as were possible with them. Fortunately, Page restrained this kind of experimentation, therefore, fans who bought *Physical Graffiti* were rewarded with twelve wonderful tracks. An electronic specialist named Roger Mayer made Page his own Fuzztone box way back in the 1960s and Page became a gadgetry buff from then on. Jimmy Page was attracted to the raw emotional atmosphere he heard in the recordings of the 1950s blues men and the gritty voice of Robert Plant frequently added to the soulful impact of the band's music. During my adolescence, the air waves were infiltrated by their deep and satisfying lyric and the intensely strong guitar, drums and bass. Taking the blues to heavier and darker levels of sound than previously heard, there was no precedent for this calibre of rock music. Songs from the following recordings are heard frequently on the radio to this date. The recordings of *Led Zeppelin* (1969), *Led Zeppelin II* (1969), *Led Zeppelin III* (1970), the untitled fourth Led Zeppelin album, and *Houses of the Holy* (1973) were recorded on the Atlantic label. The remaining Led

Zeppelin albums were recorded on their own Swan Song label: *Physical Graffiti* (1975), *Presence* (March 1976), *The Song Remains The Same* (September 1976), *In Through The Out Door* (1979), *Coda* (1982).

Led Zeppelin reigned supreme from 1973 to 1975; no band sold more concert tickets. Even in 1977 they played to 76,229 fans at the Silverdome in Pontiac, Michigan. In 1973 Superhype publishers manufactured the Led Zeppelin Songbook which contained forty songs written by Led Zeppelin band members.[12] Their mix of acoustic and electric sounds are impressive in concert. The sound of Jimmy Page is distorted and loud, it reverberates and echoes, it has a solid, electric bass line which would later come to define heavy metal, blues music. His sound is an expression of his character, deep and foreboding and yet sweet and sensible.

In August of 1973 the band's concert at Madison Square Garden in New York City was filmed and became the musical part of a film called *The Song Remains The Same* which was released in 1976. This film shows each of the band members on their home turfs in Britain receiving letters about projected tour dates. Their influential manager, Peter Grant, also has a scene in the film. The film contains nature sequences such as Robert Plant riding a horse on a beach and Jimmy Page climbing a mountain. Captured here is John Bonham, playing the drums more powerfully and erratically than anyone ever did, in a thirty minute performance of 'Moby Dick' and intermittent cuts of the film show him driving a race car rather quickly. Shown also is the erotic male swagger of Jimmy Page on stage being thin and elegant and wearing black velvets with stars and moons and astrological symbols embroidered into the trousers and a rose unto the jacket. He could not have weighed more than one hundred and forty-five pounds here, but the power, the individuality and the grace in this performance are to me like that of KRSNA. There is always a spare precision radiating from his persona; a controlled freedom of the imagination emanates through his refined facial structure always when he talks, moves or strikes his electric guitar with a violin bow then systematically points to the left then the right making an arc in the air I see a male peacock spreading his feathers. Personally, I am attracted to this particular type of quiet and restrained masculinity, but Robert Plant with all his brazen machismo, his gruff wails and big hair appealed to all of my girlfriends. One in particular recalls the film as being one big crotch shot of Robert Plant.

Perhaps the harsh criticism Led Zeppelin endured from the press for most of their career inspired loyalty from their fans. After all it is fun to like things which your parents detest and during the 1970s it was unacceptable to trust the opinions of those over the age of thirty. What inspired my loyalty, however, was watching Jimmy Page slither across the stage in *The Song Remains The Same*. His sex appeal alone would make the men who criticised him in magazines appear to be impotent and jealous old men. His acting scene in the film displays him climbing a mountain to the top, as he approaches the top he reaches his hand up toward a shadowy, Druid figure who bears the face of Page as an old man.

Adventurous Souls

Jimi Hendrix was not ahead of his time, but he was way ahead of the others intellectually.[1]

Jimmy Page

The music of Led Zeppelin begins to be imitated more and more frequently beginning in 1976 around the time of the release of their seventh album *Presence*. What knocks the listener out in this music is the expertise of the guitar player. To be sure, Jimmy Page should not be classified as a great guitar player merely because he was one of the first players of both rock and blues to enjoy the enormous success which came his way, but rather because of the music he made is one of a very few that the audience can listen to repeatedly without boredom. It is of that same peculiar strain of music as that created by Mozart and some of the New Age musical artists, which elicits new feeling and insights with each listen. Every song recorded by Led Zeppelin carries a very fully produced sound. This roundness of sound is a feature that Page had mastered by 1976 as he moved one step further in his expansion of his 'guitar army' sound. The four Englishmen of Bonham, Jones, Page and Plant whose talents varied immensely, grew together, musically, and produced an exploration on *Presence* which resulted in speed-rock, music ten years before the genre existed. The music moves very quickly and many bands have tried to duplicate its precision, heavy meaning and spooky tone. 'Royal Orleans' is a jazzy excerpt about a hotel in New Orleans where the band had previously spent some time. The last three songs of *Presence* are more in the Led Zeppelin tradition, for instance, 'Tea for One' is incredible in the blues strain of emotion and moves me personally, as much as 'Since I've Been Loving You'. A display of truly, unbelievable musical ability dominates here. With 'Nobody's Fault But Mine' it is obvious why Jimmy Page was named the world's best guitarist in 1975. The album is a statement about the individual against society which contains a soulful purpose and extreme musicianship of all band members and is a showcase of their experiences. 'Candy Store Rock' is memorable for Plant imitating Elvis Presley and describes the Los Angeles groupie scene of the 1970s. The music of Led Zeppelin was slowly being picked up by other bands at this time and the heavy metal style was becoming quite popular. The many guitar players who would follow Jimmy Page to stardom sometimes had more musical equipment than Page (they were nearly always louder) and some may have had more classical training than Page, but no matter what level of virtuosity, there is currently no heavy metal music recorded which stands up to the thirty years of recording done by Jimmy Page. Completely removed from the rock genre of the 1990s is the Eastern modality of a song like 'Kashmir'. As *Rolling Stone* writer Stephen Davis suggested in 1976, this album confirmed them as the heavy metal champions.[2]

Side one of the album *Presence* is comprised of three songs 'Achilles Last Stand', 'For Your Life' and 'Royal Orleans', but the lyrics are difficult to understand and once deciphered, the lyrics of 'Achilles Last Stand' consist of disconnected thought fragments. Phil Carson, intermediary between Atlantic records and Page during the 1980s, told me in January of 1998, when he was managing the Jason

Bonham band, that 'Candy Store Rock' was about Page and Plant retrieving drag queens and other assorted forms of groupies and servicing them in their hotel rooms after shows, or I would have never known. There is a very experimental feeling happening, the music is new sounding, but it is a long wait, until side two, before it is recognisable as Led Zeppelin music. 'Nobody's Fault But Mine' reminds us, subtly, of the great Led Zeppelin music which pre-empted *Presence*. 'Hots On For Nowhere' consists of that same language that only Led Zeppelin members themselves are capable of understanding. 'Tea for One' redeems the entire project because it is of the most improvisational type of blues music and seems heartfelt. It is as though Page suddenly remembered what he excelled at and decided to give us a taste of it. The photography on the package of the album is as colourful and interesting as the music on the vinyl.

Critics and writers were, rarely, supportive of Led Zeppelin performances, but if the band used clichés in their stage show, they were clichés of their own invention. On 6th April, 1977, Led Zeppelin performed at the Chicago Stadium in Chicago, Illinois. John Milward's *Rolling Stone* review of that concert describes the show as consisting of hard rock clichés. I found his article to be descriptive of the audience in a negative way. Milward describes the audience like this: 'most people were too dazed and confused to complain.'[3]

I guess favourites such as 'Stairway to Heaven' and 'Kashmir' were not enough to thrill writers back then, but the people I have interviewed who attended Led Zeppelin concerts in the 1970s told me that the band played sloppily at times, but audience members left a Led Zeppelin show happy and satisfied.

On 4th August, 1979, Led Zeppelin made their first concert appearance in two years at Knebworth House in

Britain's Hertfordshire. Here they added a visual spectacle of lasers to their exhilarating show as a hundred and twenty thousand people overlooked. An 11th August date was added and combined attendance for the two events was three hundred and fifty thousand people.[4]

This month also marked the release of their ninth LP, *In Through the Out Door*, which contains a self-confident creativity and a fluent stream-of-consciousness style. The layering techniques involved enable Page to have a strong rhythm guitar backing an aggressive lead guitar. 'In the Evening' is splotchy in the same manner as an impressionistic painting; there is luxuriousness and an elegant relaxation felt when listening. 'All My Love' displays the orchestral sounds Page began to incorporate into his blues music. These are combined with an acoustic guitar weaved among the metal sounding electric. The album was created at Polar Music Studios in Stockholm, Sweden. John Paul Jones worked to produce much of this recording. New imported rhythms are heard and replace earlier album's distortion and feedback. At the end of the disco era (a three year period of terrible machine-created music) came the Led Zeppelin song 'Carouselambra', an interesting, exciting and fun dance song. 'I'm Gonna Crawl' is hot, vitalisingly so and is not soon forgotten once heard. This brown paper bag packaged vinyl recording of 1979 was the last recording the band made together.

During the Renaissance, physicians believed the human body to be under astrological dominion with each part being linked to a specific sign and the sign Gemini came to be linked to the hands. The planet Mars was in Gemini at the time Page was born in January of 1944. Mars is the planet associated with energy levels in humans. When Mars is in Gemini in a natal chart there is a nervous energy which needs channelling. Page by choosing to be a guitarist channels this hand energy very creatively and constructively. In *The Song Remains the Same* there is a moment at the end of the film, during the performance of 'Whole Lotta Love', where he uses his hands to direct the sound waves in the air. The position of Mars in the air sign of Gemini indicates a restless youth and a person who will always try to communicate. The planet, Saturn, the ruler of Capricorn, his birth sign, is in Gemini also. Saturn is the planet which affects the sense of purpose and the direction one takes in life. The enormous planet Uranus also resided in Gemini in the year of 1944 and this adds a sparkling aspect to the personality of Jimmy Page which is reinforced by the other two planets there. The Moon is in Cancer, as it was in the birth chart of Jimi Hendrix. This placement bestows much artistic ability and emotional sensitivity.

Jimi Hendrix and Jimmy Page simultaneously slid into the role of Romantic rock guitarists, but Page extended this spectre by a landslide by outliving Hendrix whose guitar playing, free and loving nature, intelligent and inspirational lyrics such as those in 'Voodoo Chile', on stage pyromania, beautiful manner of dressing, and blatant efforts to prove that a modern day male guitarist is really no different from a male dog in the desire to mate with any female who proves to be available for a minute or two went far in making Hendrix the Romantic hero of the electric guitar.

To communicate in music has been the general objective of Jimmy Page, but no musical artist communicated more than Jimi Hendrix. For a variety of reasons this is so, but one of the most obvious is that Hendrix both sang and played guitar. Hendrix did a small amount of rural exploration in his short lifetime before he made the music on Electric Ladyland, in which he created a fantasy world. His lyrics are referent to other planets of which he seemed to have a knowledge. He had huge hands which controlled the guitar. His music and lyrics displayed his pervasive mental outlook. My favourite song, 'Angel', tells of love between the moon and the deep sea. His songs, in their original form were longer than some of the chapters in this book. He had much to say and a short length of time in which to say it, a boundless imagination with which to say it and he really came up the hard way whereas Sir Page found opportunities easily. If I could cite one major difference between their two personalities it would be the naive, optimism of Jimi Hendrix juxtaposed against the wise, pessimism of Jimmy Page. It is not surprising that Jimi Hendrix and Brian Jones were best friends. The two had an immense individuality and pure inspiration in common. Brian Jones formed the famous rhythm and blues band the Rolling Stones.

Jimmy Page claims to be familiar with the teachings of Pythagoras, the Greek philosopher who lived five hundred years before the birth of Christ. Pythagoras believed in a brotherhood between men and beasts and he abstained from eating animal flesh. Among his many mathematical discoveries were the notions that all things are numbers and that musical intervals depend on certain arithmetical ratios, more understandably, he showed music or pleasant sounds were created by strings or pipes which lengths are held in proportion to each other. His discovery led to the seven note scale modes. Page has a tendency to be impressed by people who are famous, especially historically well-known figures and he also has a fondness for precision which explains his interest in the theories of Pythagoras. The Pythagorean Theorum of mathematics states that in a right-angled triangle the square of the hypotenuse equals the sum of the square of the legs.[5]

1st December, 1979, the *Melody Maker* poll voted Led Zeppelin best in seven categories: Best Live Act, Band of the Year, Best Album, Top Guitarist: Jimmy Page, Top Producer: Jimmy Page, Top Composer: Led Zeppelin, and their Best Male Singer was Robert Plant.

Noise dominated much of the air waves after the disappearance of Led Zeppelin in the 1980s, but there was such a hunger for the legacy they had left behind that scores of bands containing loud playing guitarists appeared and profited by doing their best imitations of heavy metal and blues rock music. Also at this juncture, in 1981, Music Television (MTV) made its appearance and every television owner who paid for cable had access to popular music accompanied by a two or three minute video experience. The result was an overemphasis on physical appearance and stage postures of performers rather than on the musical sound. This event also divided Led Zeppelin music from other hard rock music, putting it safely and neatly in the Romantic genre. Page would not make a music video until 1993. Romantic hard rock musicians are rough and raw, they, rarely, feel the need to reassure themselves by wearing eye liner and I have yet to see a truly inspirational metal guitarist who teased and sprayed his or her hair before a performance.

The Business

Individual characters and histories are fixed by current myths and the representations of art.[1]

Sir James George Frazer

I think it best not to confuse fame with greatness in my account of guitarists who have inspired me. Female guitarist Memphis Minnie, who made her first recording in 1929, became famous, but Eric Clapton attained greatness by playing the blues to save his soul and his sanity.

In 1962 Jimmy Page played guitar in a band called Screaming Lord Sutch and the Savages at popular British nightclubs such as the White Hart Hotel in Acton and the Goldhawk Road Social Club in Shepherd's Bush. On these nights band members would hop in and out of coffins on stage. In 1964 the Kinks' producer Shel Talmy, recruited Page to professionalise the Who's first hit song 'Can't Explain'. Another rock guitarist who took his music very seriously, was Eric Clapton, who played in London-based bar bands the Roosters and Casey Jones and the Engineers before being instrumental in the band of the decade, the Yardbirds. Clapton attended the Kingston Art School, but loved blues music more than the drawing he also had a talent for, he came to be a blues guitar hero ten years before Jimmy Page became highly acclaimed.[2]

The earthier and more materialistic aspects of the personality of Jimmy Page were just beginning to be evident in 1971 and a desire to maintain a close affinity to nature began to dramatically mark his personality. His darling, Oriental-shaped eyes shone out of a face which resembled that of a porcelain beauty doll. This is no exaggeration, as the women who had sex with him throughout his tours have attested. Nature saved much of her finest handiwork for the mind and body of Jimmy Page.

Film maker Kenneth Anger, who as a child appeared in the film version of Shakespeare's *A Midsummer Night's Dream* as the Indian prince, hired Jimmy Page to create the musical soundtrack for his 1970s film *Lucifer Rising*. Page was one of four guitarists to work on the soundtrack. Kenneth Anger sought out the services of Jimmy Page by meeting him at a Los Angeles book auction. It really is amazing how naive and trusting Jimmy Page can be at times and at others so utterly, cynical and suspicious. He was flattered by Anger's recruitment of him for the film, he failed to see he was being used for his fame in promotion for the project. Hopefully, both parties got what they wanted, which was further enlightenment on their mystical paths.

Page later allowed his massive fortune to dominate his life and he used it to barricade himself from the world. On *In Through The Out Door* his altered states of mind are obvious. The damaging repercussions of the surfeit of glory this band received became extremely obvious before 1980. Raging youth, who need to dance wildly, take succour wherever they can find it. In 1980 one of the places they could find it was Germany where Led Zeppelin performed their last sets together on these dates, in these places: 17th June: Dortmund, Germany, 19th June: Cologne, Germany, 20th June: Brussels, Belgium, 21st June: Rotterdam, The Netherlands, 23rd June, Bremen, Germany, 24th June: Hanover, Germany, and 27th June:

Nuremberg, Germany, upon which date Led Zeppelin performed five songs when John Bonham passed out at his drum set mid-way through the performance. Promises were made over the speaker system that tickets held were good for all remaining performances in Germany. The band continued their touring efforts by playing in Vienna, Austria on 28th June and then appearing in Zurich, Switzerland on 29th June 29. On 2nd and 3rd July, Led Zeppelin appeared in Mannheim, Germany, on 5th July it was in Munich, and their last performance was given on 7th July in Berlin, Germany, where John Bonham was unable to complete his set and the performance concluded with Bad Company drummer, Simon Kurke.

It was appropriate that the last effort of Led Zeppelin would have an album cover displaying a bar-room, fully equipped with a drinking customer bearing a resemblance to John Bonham, who died at the age of thirty-two from alcohol poisoning and asphyxiation from choking on his own vomit. John Bonham felt the need to consume forty shots of vodka on 23rd September, 1980, his last day on earth. His gravesite is located in Rushcock, England.

The enormously powerful sound of the music of Led Zeppelin came largely from two of the four members. Robert Plant had a roar which was as loud and forceful as a mountain lion's. You really have to hear a live version of it to appreciate its primal power. John Bonham passionately banged his drums with extremely big sticks and he knew how to make music out of his drumbeats. He was superhumanly strong, but, sadly, not strong enough. He is missed and no rock drummer will ever be as adorably childlike and simultaneously, soulfully effective.

Pamela Miller, who spent time sewing shirts for Mr Page, wasted time falling in love with him and, according to her book, was quite well liked by Led Zeppelin members, wrote a documentary to tell the public about her

Los Angeles adventures with celebrities, found Page to be a heartbreaking disappointment. Page, however, fell for a beautiful, French girl named Charlotte Martin who gave him his first child, a daughter, and who also watched his occult bookstore, Equinox at 4, in Kensington. The relationship between Ms Martin and Mr Page eventually fell apart and Page gave up the bookstore in 1979.[3]

Led Zeppelin debuted at the Surrey University in 1968 and in 1974 they created their own record label: Swan Song. Six years later their party was over.

The soul of the band's effort surfaces on their last compilation, *Coda*.

When our progeny listen to the music of *Coda*, will they understand it? Did we? All of the tracks on the last release of the rock group Led Zeppelin were created between 1969 and 1978. The song 'Darlene' sounds, to us, like a tribute to Elvis Presley. 'Bonzo's Montreux' is John Bonham's drum sounds with minimal guitar distortion added by Jimmy Page. 'Ozone Baby' is singer Robert Plant talking about love so we know and accept this as the dream Led Zeppelin gave us. 'Wearing and Tearing' makes no musical or lyrical sense at all, but by this unpretension is rock music. 'We're Gonna Groove' is most exemplary of their talent, the great drums and the sensual, bass guitar played by John Paul Jones. 'Poor Tom' soothes my nerves every time I hear it and I love it here because these acoustic sounds are not often associated with the pleasurable music of Jimmy Page even though they comprise a substantial portion of his body of work. In 'I Can't Quit You Baby' we know exactly who and what we are hearing: Jimmy Page playing Willie Dixon blues Led Zeppelin style. The song 'Walter's Walk' was one of the songs the band had recorded in 1972 at the Rolling Stones' mobile Stargroves. The interior of the album jacket contains thirty-two pictures of the band and the album was mixed at Page's own Sol Studios.

On 4th December, seventy-one days after the death of their drummer, Jimmy Page, Robert Plant and John Paul Jones decided that Led Zeppelin could not continue as a band. They announced their decision to the press one week later. Later, Atlantic Records claimed Led Zeppelin owed them another record, so the remaining members dug up what they could and *Coda* was the result. Some maintain the out-takes which comprise Led Zeppelin's tenth LP, *Coda* which was released in November of 1982, is the band's sloppiest work, but the musicians' feelings for their music is what it discloses, so it turns out to be a marginally accurate replica of the different range of styles which Led Zeppelin played. This work does something much more substantial, slicing a demarcation line a mile wide into the world of music and unconsciously extends the Romantic era of music. With their musical style and by narrowly missing the MTV era Led Zeppelin comes in as the world's only heavy metal, Romantic rock band.

Gothic is a word which has been used to describe Led Zeppelin's musical work. Romantic describes their style of music more accurately, but for a moment, let us decide for ourselves if their music approaches the Gothic, a term applied to a style of architecture used in castles, houses and most European churches during the Victorian era. Gothic style was immense, intricate and imposing. Organ and keyboard instrumentals comprised background music for singers in these Gothic churches, consequently a Gothic sound would resonate loud, powerful and sombre keyboards. Led Zeppelin did have a keyboard player. Building churches and playing music are human attempts at reaching God.[4]

Engineers who worked on Led Zeppelin projects were as follows: Glyn Johns on *Led Zeppelin I*, Andrew Johns and Terry Manning on *Led Zeppelin III*, Eddie Kramer worked on *Houses of the Holy* and *Led Zeppelin II*, Keith Harwood and Jeremy Gee on *Presence*, and Ron Nevison, George Chkiantz, and Andrew Johns on *Physical Graffiti*.

Jimmy Page outgrew his fascination with Aleister Crowley, the writer, mountain climber, and self-pronounced occult scientist. However, there were plenty of bands who emulated Page later and took occultism and ran blindly with their demonic show fronts, black outfits, addictions to white, powdery drugs and hellish song lyrics. Crowley was a curious obsession of Jimmy Page, which turned into public curiosity. Rock bands Black Sabbath and, apparently, Led Zeppelin, paved the way for the Satanic heavy-metal underground movement of music that would surface during the last years of the twentieth century.

My birth path number is seven as was that of Aleister Crowley. Like Crowley I have conscientiously concerned myself with seeking truth throughout my life. Although seven is regarded as the magic number by numerologists, people whose number is seven are highly emotional. There are seven notes in the musical scale, seven days in a week, seven colours in the spectrum. Pythagoras regarded seven, not nine, as the final stage of completion in the life cycle. Seven serves as a cipher for many difficult to comprehend phenomena. In part, this is why it was delineated for a person with a seven birth path number to explain Jimmy Page to the future. The birth path number of Eric Clapton is a seven, Sir Page is a one, and Hendrix a nine. Birth numbers are figured by adding all of the numbers in a birth date. Mine are 11/28/1957.

It was during the month of November of 1967 that the entrepreneurial journalist, Jann Wenner, published his first issue of the San Francisco-based, rock magazine, *Rolling Stone*. Some influential forms of twentieth century communication began sprouting during the 1960s. It was a time of great naiveté and innocence in America, but that changed as the years went by.

During the 1970s many record executives, agents, managers, promoters and producers seduced some of their musician clients, with drugs such as cocaine and marijuana. The psychedelic drugs LSD and mescaline were not as appealing as they were during the 1960s. Luckily for us, Jimmy Page and his road crew manager knew where to get their own intoxicants consequently, Peter Grant and Jimmy Page were never compromised by record executives as many other artists have been. Neither did Page need a producer to tell him how to make a good record. From 1974 until the release of *Coda* in 1982, Page recorded on his own record label, *Swan Song*. Before 1975, Led Zeppelin had a few gold album awards, a gold record being one which sells more than five hundred thousand copies. *Led Zeppelin* went gold in July of 1969, *Led Zeppelin II* in November of 1969, *Led Zeppelin III* in October of 1970, *Led Zeppelin IV* in November of 1971, *Houses of the Holy* in April of 1973, *The Song Remains The Same* went gold in 1976 and platinum in 1977, and subsequent vinyl records made by Led Zeppelin went platinum. Led Zeppelin was Atlantic Records' largest selling act and they also broke all box office records set before them.

In September of 1975, Bruce Springsteen released *Born to Run* which became the recording industry's first record to receive the platinum award, a platinum record being one which sells one million copies or more. One year later *Frampton Comes Alive* sold more than any other record in the history of the industry, thus commercialising the industry even further.[5]

The present rate of cost for a CD is $16.98 and a tape cassette around $10.98. The Japanese and Europeans were the first to use CDs and it was 1983 when Americans began utilising the better sound that CDs offer.

Symphonies, Melodies and the Love Music of my Life

That in an April sunbeam's fleeting glow
Fulfils its destined though invisible work.[1]

Lord Byron

The Classical style of music contains a highly, flexible rhythm and tone colour and is variable in dynamics and volume. In the Classical orchestra the woodwind and brass instruments were given clearly defined roles. It is easy to identify Classical music as opposed to Romantic because the former is emphatic of perfection and beauty. Romantic music heats a listener's blood, is uplifting and takes us somewhere other than where we are. The eighteenth-century European philosophical movement which accompanied Classical music, the enlightenment, was one characterised by rationalism, an impetus towards learning and a spirit of scepticism and empiricism in social and political thought. Neo-classicism was first an eighteenth-century movement in the arts returning to Greek and Roman models and then a twentieth-century movement involving a return to the style and form of older music, particularly eighteenth-century music.

Pianoforte virtuoso Franz Liszt wrote in Vienna in the nineteenth century and conducted what was considered music of the future and his music may well be considered futuristic today. High quality lasts a long, long time. His 'Liebestraum' frees up the imagination. The amount of learning Franz Liszt did which enabled him to create his Romantic music is astonishing. To musicians of his day, he was very helpful in helping them to achieve their goals and his music is full of sunlight. He was born in Hungary in 1811 and at twelve years of age was a concert pianist. In his middle age he became a secular priest.[2]

During the previous age of absolutism (which names an ideal of music purity), chorales, and their preludes, oratorios, hymns and church cantatas were very popular forms of music. An oratorio is an opera on a religious subject. The sonata was developed by the Classical composers and the sonata form is used in almost all the first movements of their symphonies. The sonata form contains exposition, development and recapitulation. Sonatas typically contain three or four movements of which this type of musical composition was mastered long ago and has certainly not been rivalled since.

The work of Hector Berlioz, who was born, in 1803, has had great influence on composers. Lasting favourites composed by Berlioz are his Fantastic Symphony which includes a 'Witches Round Dance' and a funeral march for Hamlet. Berlioz was considered an orchestra master and, apparently, a genius by nineteenth-century composers because he engineered programme music and he treated timbre in a unique way. English composer and Professor of Music Sir Edward Elgar wrote an oratorio called 'The Dream of Gerontius' and 'The Apostles' and concert overture 'In the South' were performed at a three day Elgar festival at Covent Garden, London in March of 1904. His is the kind of soothing religious music I love to hear and his symphonies fall into the Romantic category. Elgar composed 'Pomp and Circumstance' which is often played during graduations and at other ceremonial occasions.

Of all the Romantic musicians, Nicolo Paganini, is the one to which we can, realistically, draw comparisons with Jimmy Page. Paganini began to play the mandolin at the age of five, after a couple of years he began to play the violin exclusively then in 1796 he began to play the guitar as well. He lived from 1782 until 1840 and became one of the greatest Italian composers and wrote many sonatas for the violin and the guitar. He travelled much in Europe in his concert-giving career. Although he was creative, he became renowned for his technical wizardry, he knew how to conduct and conducted an orchestra in a performance of a piece by Rossini in 1821. Paganini toured to excess in spite of ill health. One of his most dramatic on stage effects was the left-hand pizzicato, he composed his own music, and was said by all to be the best violin player who had ever lived. Both Page and Paganini broke the third finger of their left hand. Paganini in March of 1834 and Page in 1975.

Freedom is not a universal mainstay, it is a privilege. I think freedom is the greatest gift one human being can give to another. American citizens who dislike America should collect themselves together and move to China. Freedom is wealth just as wealth is freedom and the privileges Americans enjoy today were earned in the eighteenth century by people who thought freedoms were worth fighting for. Without artistic, religious and political freedoms there would have been no 'Für Elise' and the members of Led Zeppelin would have had to conform to the standards of their society. Instead hundreds of musicians have been able to build upon, explore and expand the music of the past. Everything good in the world today came to fruition as a result of man's free will and his ability to express it.

James Marshall Hendrix was born on 27th November, 1942. He was a patriotic American citizen who served in the US army as a paratrooper, far advanced of everyone in his guitar playing performances and his exhibitions on stage were emotional torrents of energy which included setting his Stratocaster on fire and physically humping his Marshall amplifier. Some of his sexually energised shows were recorded on video. In 1966 he went to London, England to play. Of course, the British audiences were just as shocked as anyone. Most everyone who watched him on stage must have done so for the first time with their mouth wide open. Can you imagine the stoic Jimmy Page and Mick Jagger, who were on their way at this time, watching Jimi Hendrix blasting out 'Wild Thing'?

His last official studio album, *Electric Ladyland*, from 1968 included 'Voodoo Child' and 'Rainy Day Dream Away' and was sonically awe-inspiring. I think many, many guitarists were relieved when Hendrix left the planet in 1970, because that meant that they could trudge slowly on as stars of the show. Page and Hendrix were the most technically innovative guitarists. The public use of whammy bars, feedback, distortion and war wah pedals began with Jimmy Page though in his first band Neil Christian and the Crusaders before he became a studio musician.

I have heard many a guitarist say he wished he could play like Jimi Hendrix who also sang while he played. His voice reached out to me in a provocative yet childlike way and told me it is acceptable to be intense, intelligent, passionate, creative, sexual and honest. His song lyrics were thoughtful, beautiful and profound and they blew all the dust out of the way just as did his left-handed guitar playing. 'Purple Haze', 'Hey Joe' and 'The Wind Cries Mary' are often played on the radio quite often in the 1990s. Jimmy Page hangs the thumb of his rather large hand sloppily over the bridge of the acoustic guitar while he plays, as did Hendrix.

So far I have tried to describe what Hendrix did and told a little about the way he sounded and I have still done little because to me, he was the snappiest and most colourful dresser ever. He wore all of my favourite colours: purple or orange knee length velvet coats and gold velvet jeans and a red bandanna around his head. Jimi Hendrix was definitely not in command of the cold charm and inwardly seething and determined charisma of Jimmy Page, but nonetheless a force to be reckoned with and a guitar player that the world has yet to come to terms with. Seeing and hearing Jimi Hendrix on video is like being hit in the head by a flying saucer from outer space. Only he was a human being and he left so soon it was heartbreaking. He holds a very special place in the American heart. These are the three studio albums which he completed during his lifetime: *Are You Experienced?*, *Axis: Bold As Love*, *Electric Ladyland*, *Smash Hits*, *Otis Redding/Jimi Hendrix Experience at Monterey*, and *Band of Gypsies* were montages of his music which were released during his lifetime and dozens of compilations of his music have been released since his death.

With the death of Jimi Hendrix in September of 1970, his brand of electric church music turned into theatrical rock which dominated the 1970s. The focus of music drifted from the earlier decade's folksong based on society's problems and the civil rights movements of the 1960s took a back seat to 1970s government corruption. High unemployment and high rates of inflation turned many young people onto entrepreneurial paths of employment of which music was but one. 1970 ushered in Crosby, Stills, Nash and Young's protest song about the murder of four students by officials at Kent State University. This song, 'Ohio', was pretty much the end of the love and peace movement in music. I remember a circus type atmosphere and a lyrical emphasis on an escape from reality. Drug addiction on a larger scale became a growing facet of American society. In India, opium use was legal, but not alcohol intake. In America, to use marijuana, heroin or cocaine was against the law. This law was viewed by many youths at that time as a hypocritical law since many of their parents took tranquillisers and drank coffee and alcohol.

By 1977 Jimmy Page had copied all of the black blues guitarists to the point of virtuosity. Their talents were immense in a traditional, yet stormy way. Otis Rush whose 1956 version of 'I Can't Quit You Baby' began his impressive recording career, was emulated by Eric Clapton, Stevie Ray Vaughan and copied by Sir Page. The solos of Page and Rush are almost identical on 'I Can't Quit You'. The guitarist most emulated by Hendrix, Clapton, Page and Beck, however, was Muddy Waters who sang as well as played the blues.

Another guy who was emulated constantly and by nearly everybody was John Lee Hooker, who was born in Clarksdale, Mississippi in 1917. He had a hit song with 'Crawling King Snake' in 1949 and Plant named one of his blues bands after it. Hooker performed at folk music festivals, Blues Festivals during the 1960s. His music was featured in the Steven Spielberg film *The Colour Purple*. One of the most important things for him, musically, was to remember the great blues artists like John Hammond, Van Morrison and B B King. He had an amazing abundance of names which he recorded under, such as Texas Slim, Delta John, John Lee Cooker and John Lee Booker. He filled the blues waves with charming and meaningful lyrics and his favourite guitar is made by the Gibson manufacturer.[3]

When I was eight years old I performed a daily song and dance routine with my five-year-old cousin Victoria. We had a repertoire of eight or nine songs by Motown artists which we sang on the fireplace to the delight of our parents. My favourite artist to imitate was Marvin Gaye. One of an abundant array of creative singers of the 1970s, his songs were still being written for him not by him in the summer of 1968. Victoria and I sang the songs 'Ain't Nothing Like the Real Thing', 'Ain't No Mountain High Enough' and 'You're All I Need to Get By' which he sang with the darling Tammi Terrell. These songs were fun and the vocals strong in the rhythm and blues manner. Singer Marvin Gaye made the listener feel his lyrics. His song 'Too Busy Thinking About My Baby' came later and by this time we had extended our repertoire to include 'Build Me Up Buttercup' by the Foundations, 'Lady Willpower' by Gary Puckett and the Union Gap and 'Hello, I Love You' by the Doors. However, by 1970 Marvin Gaye reached to the depths of his creative soul and the results were on the LP *What's Going On?*, a profound look at humanity. Contained here are the saddest and most thoughtful songs such as 'Abraham Martin and John' and 'What's Going On?'. He followed this LP with *Let's Get It On* and both are serious blues masterpieces performed by the most handsome and gifted male soul-singer of the twentieth century.

Songs by Motown artists showed a wellspring of song-writing creativity, were never folksy, were slightly mechanical and well orchestrated (in the manner of Phil Spector), but these songs were soul and blues at its most innocent time. This beautiful, soul sound of the 1960s is what instilled in me a love for music so by the time Led Zeppelin released their fifth LP in March of 1973, I knew what I liked in music and 'Dancing Days', 'The Ocean' and 'Over the Hills and Far Away', the songs on *Houses of The Holy* were it. The songs of the 1971 *Led Zeppelin IV* and those from *Houses of the Holy* rather run together in theme continuity and it is amazing how modern these two recordings sound in the 1990s. The four songs from *IV*:

'Misty Mountain Hop', 'Four Sticks', 'Going To California' and 'When The Levee Breaks' round out and conclude Led Zeppelin's psychedelic, folk, hard-rock, blues phase. Their first five LPs were made before their music became heavy metal. The 1975 double LP *Physical Graffiti* marks the beginning of heavy metal music.

All this talk of music has left an opening in which to address the ghost of Jimmy Page, the person we feel in the music, but the one he tries to hide from us when he is on a stage. We know him as a hard-working individual; the massive tours and the flawless execution illustrated in his music show us many hours of work. His industriousness and tenacity are how, his realistic and serious outlook on life is why he clung so tenaciously to his goal of being the most versatile guitarist of all time. His rise and advancement in the music business have been a result of untiring effort and devotion to his vocation. Part of what he does not show on the stage, and in public are his emotional strength and affectionate nature. His domesticity, family spirit, simplicity, economy and impressionability are the delicately, sweet aspects of his personality which are seen only by family members and friends, but if one listens well enough to *Houses of the Holy* these are visible. He is not detached from his emotions and there is an interrelationship between his stomach and his emotional state. He is tough and shrewd enough to solve difficult problems and ambition has fuelled all of his activities in life. He considers himself worthy of payment for his work because he knows the concentration, thoroughness, endurance and patience which he gives to his musical work. Jimmy Page has always had the power to wish.

Traditionally in America much importance has been placed on achievement and improving one's status. The pressure that Americans cope with to climb up the economic ladder many times requires a fair amount of sacrifice of individuality and hence they sometimes fail to cultivate their own well-thought-out methods of independence. The pressures in England are similar, but for some reason, the majority of their artists display an interesting individuality.

James Page explored the conventions and sought to overcome them. He did this with a bit of borrowing from the then known American blues players, but mostly just by being focused on playing his guitar. The imaginative art work on every Led Zeppelin album cover is exemplative of a free thinking and artistic temperament. After much world travel and success he trusted his own thoughts enough to act on any of them and through this ability to act he has been aided in the struggles encountered with record companies. His meditative nature enables him to spend days in reflection. Page has a natural ability to exert some authority and to do what he wants to do.

From 1969 until the time of the death of drummer, John Bonham, in 1980, the employment of Jimmy Page was entirely with Led Zeppelin. This would change but it would not be an easy or painless transition for him. Suddenly, Page had difficulty in synthesising his perceptions which enabled him to gain his own unique, musical perspectives. Part of what he realised during the mid 1980s was everyone was living their own life except for him and it would be a long decade before he would be able to be the great artist again. Page paid for losing his friend, John Bonham, in more ways than one and members of the press were persistently rude in circulating spooky rumours about Page. Implied was that Page and his occult interests caused the accidental death to occur at the house of Jimmy Page. Losing John Bonham led to Jimmy Page losing his direction for a very long time.

His new work after Led Zeppelin consisted of music for a motion picture soundtrack called *Death Wish II*. Released in 1982, the project was not his own idea. His neighbour was directing the film. The soundtrack consists of macabre and interesting sounds like those present in the darker sequences of *The Song Remains The Same*. Musicians from the Hare Krishna sect have a small part in the film. The musicianship of Jimmy Page adds some substance to an otherwise intolerably violent film and he proves to have a knack for this musical soundtrack type of work.

His contributions were also used on the *Death Wish III* sound track.

In 1985 Page's new band formation, The Firm, produced a self-titled CD. Most of the songs on *The Firm* which co-stars Paul Rodgers are reminiscent of songs Rodgers sang with his previous band. The songs are brief and they move in a predictable and rather clockwise manner. 'Radioactive' became the hit single from this package. 'Midnight Moonlight' is an attractive song in a soothing tone. The band plays an old Mann/Well/Spector tune called 'You've Lost That Lovin' Feeling'. 'Money Can't Buy' is the most musically innovative of this, the first of The Firm's musical products. The name of the band implies a business and I get the feeling that this group was little more than a business transaction for its members, but the personality of Paul Rodgers and Jimmy Page's rhythmic ingenuity and unmistakable artistry show through here. The first song from their second effort, *Mean Business*, is 'Fortune Hunter'. The usually ornate guitar effects of Jimmy Page are few here, but the special beauty only he is capable of creating shines through on 'Dreaming' and 'Spirit of Love' is inspirational in a darling and childlike way. This 1986 release makes a statement against the hardness of the world's prevailing economic forces and 'Live in Peace' is powerful both lyrically and musically.

From the inception of the band on throughout the production of *The Firm* and *Mean Business*, this band was only a vehicle for Jimmy Page to get to where he needed to be and was made before he jumped to the creation of a much larger type of music. These albums are expressive of the economic climate of his native land at the time. It is as though he suddenly viewed his country as it really was, in all its economic despair and put this observation into these works. The Firm toured the United States and they played at Madison Square Garden in New York in May of 1985. This band formation of Page, Rodgers, Franklin and Slade did not allow Page or Rodgers to draw upon their many hit song, repertoires of the 1970s so their concerts were not as musically full as they could have been if each would have played songs from their past, but for fans of Jimmy Page, I am sure, these concert nights added up to a great amount of fun.

His solo effort titled *Outrider* was released in 1988, it sold enough copies to go gold and it earned Jimmy Page a Grammy nomination. He does not say much in this recording, but when he does his statements serve to show that he is most probably struggling with an elegant lifestyle and a still strong desire to make good music. There is a duality of feeling present here and this is reflected in the occasionally, ambivalent guitar playing of Jimmy Page and by the presence of vocals by Robert Plant on the song 'The Only One'. Perhaps he desired to weave this web of cheerfulness which only Robert Plant could provide; the song is extremely upbeat. Singing on the first two songs is John Miles and on three others is Chris Farlow whose voice is warm and strong. 'Hummingbird' is a ballad with wonderful guitar antics. Most touching is the fact that Jason Bonham, the son of the late Led Zeppelin drummer, John Bonham, plays the drums on most of these songs. I obtain so much pleasure from listening to this rhythm and blues music. It would be five years from the release of

Outrider before the good breeding and charming talent of James Page would take him to an even higher level of art.

In August of 1988 Jimmy Page had stomach surgery.[4]

Concert reviews for the concert Page gave at Knight Center in Miami in early September of 1988 were all quite favourable. He played 'Stairway to Heaven' to an awe-struck audience who sang the lyrics for him and vocalist John Miles. Jason Bonham played drums, Durban Leverde played bass guitar and the concert lasted over two hours. Page played intermittent slices from his entire twenty-six year career. Though few ever gave Page the credit to rise from the ashes of Led Zeppelin he ascended spectacularly from them on this night in his own beautiful way.

The mysterious urgency and intensity to even the most superficial and evanescent phenomena is not a personality trait present in everyone, but this urgency to excel helps Page make the evolution which takes place in his personality during the 1980s. By this time in his life he learned that success develops from building on the knowledge accumulated in the past. He slowly realised only he could live his life and some of his realisations occurred because he felt a freedom and luxury in being a solo artist which he never allowed himself with Led Zeppelin.

William James explained carefully in his *The Principles of Psychology* that this type of independence is crucial for a strong self identity. By this time Page had overcome the inbred sociological tendencies which tend to keep people involved in a struggle of gaining wealth at the expense of self-realisation. His past enabled him to be thoughtful about his future and there were vast possibilities in his new life outside of the rock group Led Zeppelin.

As many writers have previously noted, English people have a strong common sense in their nature and they are unusually economical and realistic. With this typically non-dream like state of mind the English people have created some of the world's greatest literature. They crave utility and they produce useful things such as music, literature, and fair teacups. Their policemen, called bobbies, do not carry guns. In America that idea is unfathomable, but this fact goes far in explaining the wonder and innocence of the music of Jimmy Page. Unfortunately, he had developed a drug dependency during the 1970s, but he began his road to recovery and some level of sobriety in 1983, after his performance at the ARMS benefit in London.[5]

On 19th October, 1987 world stock markets turned downward following a collapse of stock prices in the United States. London and Tokyo were most affected by this crash. In November of 1987 Vincent Van Gogh's painting, Irises, sold for $53.9 million at an auction at Sotheby's in New York City. Andres Segovia, who played guitar for nearly eighty years, died in Madrid at the age of ninety-four on 2nd June, 1987.

Jimmy Page became an unapproachable icon and for a number of seasons, during the 1980s, he retreated to his many subterranean hobbies. Plant and Page performed at Atlantic Records' fortieth anniversary gala at Madison Square Garden in May of 1988. In November of 1988 Jimmy Page played guitar in concert at the Frank Erwin Center in Austin, Texas during his solo *Outrider* tour. The power of his talent and the classy way in which he exhibited his music throughout this tour created a whole new legion of fans of Jimmy Page. Page had dived head first into the music business twenty-five years earlier and he had always approached the music business as one of commerce and craft. First as a studio musician, then as a producer, songwriter and as a performing artist whose performances are clearly marked by his imposing musicianship. During a hiatus from the public eye he married Patricia Ecker, in 1985, and he would remain in marital bliss with her for nine years. His life slowed down and he lived out a particularly happy and relaxing time.

Country music was topping the charts in 1988 as were songs by performers George Michael, Madonna, Aerosmith, Def Leppard and Guns and Roses. *Outrider* peaked in the charts at number twenty-six. On the 1988 Monsters of Rock tour the band Van Halen covered Led Zeppelin's 'Rock and Roll' during their set.

The Absolute Best

Please excuse me while I tend to how I feel.

Metallica

Spontaneity and independence designate all great artists and musicians beginning with Beethoven to Wagner, from Raphael to Picasso, and a wild independence marks the career of Jimmy Page from its very bud. In January of 1990 I began work on my English degree and commenced my association with the University of Nevada, Las Vegas. I simultaneously quit playing guitar, deciding that with Page and Clapton on this earth my wasting time with a guitar was pointless. At this same time Jimmy Page was hunting down original, Led Zeppelin recordings and working on the *Led Zeppelin Remasters* with John Paul Jones. This work resulted in a collection of fifty-four Led Zeppelin songs on four CDs and was released in November of 1990. By finding the original tape recordings and putting them into a new CD format, Jones and Page enhanced the sound of the original Led Zeppelin songs. Three hard-to-find Led Zeppelin songs: 'Travelling Riverside Blues', 'White Summer', and 'Hey, Hey What Can I Do?' were also made available on this new compilation.

I respect and admire people who, like myself, stubbornly go their own way no matter what the odds. Eric Clapton, who was born one year later than Page in the same part of England, has been focused on playing blues music all of his adult life and as a result of this focus his music takes the listener to an interesting world where feelings matter. The goal of Jimmy Page has always been to be as versatile a guitarist as possible, of Clapton, to play the blues devoutly. The two have reached their respective mountain peaks. In 1992 Eric Clapton put out two recordings: *Unplugged* and *Tears in Heaven*. In 1993 he won six Grammy Awards for this heart-wrenching music: Record: Eric Clapton, *Tears In Heaven*, Rock Song: EC with Jim Gordon: 'Layla', Song: 'Tears In Heaven', Male Rock Vocalist: Eric Clapton, Male Pop Vocalist: Eric Clapton, Album: Eric Clapton, *Unplugged*.[1]

To be honest, no one has equalled the blues obsession of Eric Clapton, oh, all right maybe Buddy Guy, but in a more obscure way. Clapton does not seem to even record songs unless they are a result of profound inspiration or heartbreak. He covered reggae artist, Bob Marley's, 'I Shot the Sheriff'. *Tears in Heaven* album was a result of his own tormented grief over the accidental, loss of his baby son. However, Eric Clapton is a rock superstar of the highest echelon and in a world hungry for celebrities Clapton is the real thing, he had setbacks and heartbreaks from the very beginning of his life as he kept forcing his way through in his own 'Slowhand' way.

Jimmy Page, who sleepily goes through life without too many traumas or hardships, met professionally with David Coverdale, in New York, in 1992, after Coverdale's agent arranged a meeting for the two. Page hung out with Coverdale in Lake Tahoe. I spotted Page hanging out at Caesar's Tahoe playing dollar slot machines more than once while I vacationed up there. Page was married then, and he loved to compose songs alongside his three-year-old baby boy. Coverdale and Page got involved in musical projects together. At the Lawlor Events Center in May of 1991, Poison (the name of a band who tried desperately to be popular) headlined. During the concert Jimmy Page and David Coverdale mounted the stage and performed a song. Before the concert was over, Jimmy Page fell through an opening in the stage floor and injured his arm. Just a typical, intoxicated, night out for him I suppose, or maybe all of the band's smoke and fireworks made him lose his balance.

Fans of talented musicians do not require their heroes to wear makeup or have fog in the background while they play. Great music is sufficient to dazzle, shock, inform, uplift, impress, emote and recreate. Stage effects and pyrotechnics are nice if good music is present, but if the sound of music is absent, these cannot replace it. Women are similar to men in that we want to have social experiences which mean something and we do not want to be insulted intellectually any more than we want to be hurt emotionally. We are all individuals so watching people who behave as individuals and not clones of a performer we saw on a previous night is important. The music is the most important aspect of a musical concert. Tattoos and leather I can see on my way to the grocery store, it is entirely unnecessary for me to attend a concert event to see them. I can think of nothing more unpleasant than watching a performer with a total body tattoo. Contemplating the mind/body split which would have to accompany that type of cosmetic process would be more than enough to send one's mind off a performance. I want to feel as exhilarated after a concert as I do after I run with my golden retriever. I have been more rebellious in my lifetime than any rock star. I want to feel the burn of their rebellion not witness some guitar player doing his job. When uneducated, untrained and unpractised people play musical instruments, their sound takes on a tone of artificiality as superficial as their face makeup. Jimmy Page never needed mascara.

Excitement constitutes great rock music and people who are serious about life, yet love to entertain others while having a good time are an interesting type. Page falls into this self-directed category, as did the famous trumpet player, Harry James. I know quite a bit about the life and person of Harry James, who was born in 1916. As is usually the case with great music, the tone it sets in society is what is important. Tommy Dorsey, Jimmy Dorsey and their respective orchestras, Benny Goodman, Artie Shaw, Bob Crosby, Glenn Miller, Duke Ellington, Jimmie Lunceford, Harry James, Buddy Rich, Gene Krupa, Woody Herman and Stan Kenton were individuals who had mastered their musical instruments. From 1935 until 1948, a time most commonly referred to as the Big Band Era, listening to music became an exciting, social, dancing experience for many. Studies on the relationship between music and painting date far before the Romantic Movement in art and literature, which thought music had the potential to explore other world spiritual purity. The Big Band era did not glimpse this other world, but musicians of the 1960s began to take music apart and put it back together so as to help us conceive of a better realm. The music of Page usually approaches the spiritual dimension most often because of its simple heartfelt emotion, improvisation and carefully graded variations of dark and light, loud and not so loud, and abrasive as well as soothing sounds. These contrasts comprise the major differences between the albums *Led Zeppelin II* and *Led Zeppelin III* and the 1988 *Outrider* and the 1993 *Coverdale Page*.

Jimmy Page, as a child, was intelligent enough to perceive the world as a scary, threatening place in spite of his adoring parents. Their adoration of him convinced him he was special. Consequently, through his hard work and good intentions he made an especially significant offering of music. His private musical life, the one in which he most often creates, is one of contemplation and concentration. His songs are not created while partying with the band, with the exception of *Led Zeppelin III*, and are contrived and perfected in solitude, but yet the listener is always approached. Inspirational is the fact that listening to his music never makes the listener feel the guitarist is jerking off.

Some popular music does not strike the universal soul note as does that Page plays in 'That's The Way' which states how love feels for everyone and the listener is invited to join the performer. His peculiar type of talent derives from an extroverted outlook not an introverted, me, me, me attitude. In 'That's The Way' the solo is performed against a backwash of his own acoustic instrumentals. The substance of much hard rock music is dependent on over driving the amplifier that brings about signal compression and distortion. With that volume comes a powerful sound and with the major portion of metal music today constitutes the power. Oh, some guitarists know how to tap their fingers quickly on the fret with the right hand while performing the (by 1978) old hammer-on technique, but few approach true artistry in hard rock music. Which brings us naturally to the *Coverdale Page* CD. 'Shake My Tree' shows the speedy playing of Page. In this the first song from the CD, it is the intricacy and the rapidity of his notes that you notice first and then you hear a spacious symbiosis of the vocals with the guitar. Page pulls greatness out of yet another singer. What is profound here is the listener is not privy to the spadework that was done behind the scenes, but what you hear is perfect nonetheless, and the singer makes you believe he means what he is saying. Jump over to electric guitar work on 'Waiting On You', in which the music makes you feel the lyrics. He is waiting so the song is accordingly drudging; Coverdale says he is sinking, drowning, waiting, dedicated. There are exceptionally, clarified and perfectly crisp drum sounds on this one. The players know what they are doing and it is not party time in the studio. I admire the perfectionism of David Coverdale here because he really nails the whole project down by hiring the two backup singers, Tommy Funderburk and John Sambataro to fill in any gaps. Painting in song is 'Take Me For A Little While'. Song four: 'Pride and Joy', five: 'Over Now' and six are transitional in that they take you to the other part of the CD. It is as though they are kidding all of a sudden when all four guys sing in unison on 'Feeling Hot'. I love to hear Jimmy Page brag and, thankfully, he does it just often enough to keep me in line. On page fifty-seven of the May 1993 issue of *Guitar World* he is quoted as saying: 'My standards are so high that I always want to see if I can top myself'. I am sure it is obvious to listeners of his music that he has high standards. Here he is making reference to his efforts to perfect his solo on 'Don't Leave Me This Way', song nine, which is the real Page and is a fine exhibition of Page as electric, blues man. The notes he plays here are fearful and they add emotional charge to the lyrics David Coverdale smokily screams. The two feign lovesickness here, for the sake of musical art and the result stays with the listener after the music ends. Page is expressing his desires on this CD, his passions, and he knows, from experience, he is capable of willing his way through the universe. Coverdale and Page disclosed much of their personalities in this music. This guitar music speaks to me in a personal way and it tells me that the two have exercised self-control at times, but have lived their lives in a very real, spontaneous, childlike and feeling way. Is there anything more Romantic than that? In 'Absolution Blues' the lyrics beg forgiveness for the thousand or so girls the two have bedded during their lifetimes. Page and Coverdale are attached to the world in a very, emotional and generous way. This CD far extends the heavy-metal, rock tradition originated by Jimmy Page two decades earlier. Coverdale sings passionately, he does not wail, scream or clamour and all of the songs here make the listener take notice of him. 'Waiting on You' is an honest love song. Next heard is Page's mastery of the arpeggio in the sorrowful strains of 'Take Me For a Little While'. Page and Coverdale are reminiscing about friends they lost, possibly Tommy Bolin and John Bonham. Strength and precision, mainstays belonging to Jimmy Page are used by him on a dulcimer and are the first apparent sounds of 'Pride and Joy'. Love gone sour is the theme of 'Over Now' and the song is such an interesting weave of different orchestrations that their effect is breathtaking. Lyrically, the song wants to get even for a love gone wrong. 'Take a Look at Yourself' is a song of love, hope and promise. It seems Coverdale has fully recovered from the broken heart suffered on song five. Sir Page plays better and more confidently than ever before. Orchestral and violin sounds are prevalent. The music on this CD shows Coverdale and Page to be capable of lovely artistic expression and the result is a durable work of art. The guitar work is extremely, technically, innovative and fast. Variations here are plentiful. The Page methods of guitar playing are regarded by many successful and well-known guitarists as uniquely his own, such as the guitar string hammer-ons and pull offs present on his first albums and nobody plays a chord played in arpeggio better than James Patrick Page. 'Easy Does It' begins with an acoustic twelve-string guitar and the song contains many layers. It begins calmly and has a beautiful melody, is light, happy and does not display the intense excitement of his earlier blues songs even though shadows and depth are present. This song is subtly metal. His superior studio production capabilities are well known and his layering techniques comprise the music here.

'Feeling Hot' is a boys night out type of fun song and I get a kick out of it every time I hear it. The songs 'Absolution Blues', 'Waiting on You' and 'Whisper a Prayer For the Dying', written by both Coverdale and Page, were the first creative efforts by Jimmy Page in the 1990s in which he knew for sure that he not only lived up to his previously high artistic standards, but definitely surpassed them.

Robert Plant vocalised extreme jealousy about this CD and in more than one interview he called Coverdale, David Coverversion meaning Page had only used David Coverdale because he had long, blond hair and according to Robert Plant, Coverdale also stole all of his stage moves. Pretty petty, but it just goes to prove the old adage: the bigger they are the harder they fall. Plant said he passed the vacancy left by himself on to Coverdale, but that became a lie because Plant accompanied Page right back out on the road, within two years of the release of *Coverdale Page*.

David Coverdale presents himself immaculately on stage and has worked just as hard as Plant at cultivating a singing career and when I heard Robert Plant sing Coverdale's 'Shake My Tree' at the MGM Grand Garden, I knew Coverdale sang that particular song much better. Let's just call a spade a spade and say that any show in which Jimmy Page appears is going to result in him being the star, because of his strong and unique talent, his astute business sense and his priority for organisation.

The beauty of the *Coverdale Page* CD comes, partially, from the themes of most of the songs being based on a sort of courtly love. This singer is a human being singing not a gyrating, sex machine that wants to have sex with the whole front row of an audience. Every post-pubescent girl who hears these songs thinks they are being sung to her and to her alone. If that is not an intelligent marketing strategy, I do not know of one. Apparently, Coverdale and Page were discouraged from touring behind their CD, but the group made seven appearances in Japan with Brett Tuggle on keyboards, Guy Pratt on bass and Denny Carmassi on drums. Personally, I would have flown as far as Richmond, England to see the two in concert, but Asian countries frighten me. Hopefully, one day me and my legions of female comrades will get a chance to set the record straight about the appeal of David Coverdale singing with Jimmy Page. The Coverdale/Page group also made a video of the song 'Pride and Joy' in February of 1993. Page played harmonica on this song. Coverdale credited Page with having the most intense overview of anyone he had ever worked with. That is an accurate assessment of the huge Romantic vision of Jimmy Page, who keeps a journal in which he logs his studio procedures. The *Coverdale Page* project took nine months to complete. It was with David Coverdale that the guitar work of Jimmy Page was brought into the 1990s. Like the work of the earliest Romantic composers, Chopin, Mendelssohn, Schumann, and Berlioz, the sentimental expressions on Coverdale/Page are powerful.[2]

I wanted my reader to know who Jimmy Page was. By analysing his music I discovered him. In 1988 *Rolling Stone* writer, David Fricke, called Page the high priest of heavy metal. Now I am calling him the greatest guitar player who ever lived because of the way his music has transcended all such boundaries and extended the Romantic genre of music. It is my nature to communicate honestly so it is just that I would tell the tale of man who tried through hard work in an honest way, to impress a world with his carefully cultivated musical talent. While he did this I listened carefully for twenty years…

Some people, especially creative ones need a huge expanse of space in order to flourish. Jimmy Page set out in his youth, to get things done. Before he performed on stage he did many a great performance off stage. Marianne

Faithfull, in *An Autobiography*, told what she knew of Jimmy Page and how he got interesting with pop star Jackie DeShannon. After creating a famous name for himself he managed to fall in love once or twice. Most specifically, in the 1970s with Charlotte Martin and in the 1980s with Patricia Ecker. He is always concerned about his children and their welfare and he does very well in providing for them. Doubtless this truth may not be as engrossing as some of the tirades in diaries which have included him in their tales, but with Jimmy Page, business and family come first and he tends to keep his private life very private.

The leader of Led Zeppelin took his responsibilities of leadership at home just as seriously as he did in his band of musicians. He was born to lead and he always realised the value of his relationships with people. He has been astonishingly conservative lately, considering the fact that it was he who inspired hundreds of wild, young boys to play the guitar. A small fine for drug use in the early 1980s and a thousand dollar fine for smoking on an aeroplane in May of 1995 have been the extent of his run-ins with the legal system.

His material acquisition intercepted his spiritual growth at certain times in his youth, but when taking his whole life and art into perspective, he was way ahead of the crowd, spiritually, anyway. He has been cautious with his emotions and has been sensible and reserved with his money. He followed a vegetarian diet long before it became fashionable. His emotions and love as a young adult were directed to the world rather than to one specific individual. He is very idealistic and spiritual in regards to love. He is introspective and inhibited during interviews, but he is dramatic and theatrical on stage. With his friends he is loyal, generous and exuberant. He has been lucky and his enthusiastic and optimistic nature has added to his good fortune.

Community

Music has the power to ease tension within the heart and to loosen the grip of obscure emotions. Music is serious and holy and can construct a bridge to the unseen.[1]

I Ching

The most positive aspect of the rock music industry surfaced in the uncanny ability of famous recording artists to perform so as to raise money to benefit needy people. The original of these huge musical events occurred on 1st August, 1971, at which George Harrison and other famous musicians began two concerts for Bangla Desh at New York's Madison Square Garden. Phil Spector recorded the event, Apple records executive, Pete Bennett, promoted it and Hollywood film producer, Saul Swimmer filmed it. All of which was simple. To get food and medical supplies to the war torn Bangla Desh, however, was a very complicated matter. There were tax men, record retailers and bunches of other people wanting money from the event, which raised fifteen million dollars.[2]

In 1984 others tried to aid starving people including many British rock stars and the event was called Band Aid. Twenty-two million people were starving in Ethiopia at 1984 and because of the seventeen year drought and the actions of shady, political leaders there seemed no relief in sight for these people. In England, as one Irish singer Bob Geldof watched the news in the winter of 1984, the

Ethiopian people were being shown to be dying of starvation in water-deprived deserts where temperatures reached a hundred and twenty degrees. Geldof quickly wrote a song called 'Do They Know It's Christmas?', then organised some famous British musicians and singers to sing it and eleven million dollars was raised for relief of famine in Ethiopia.

Later, forty-five American singers recorded a song called 'We Are The World'. This song was initially played by five thousand radio stations, simultaneously around the globe on 5th April, 1985. Created in an effort to raise money for starving people in Sudan, Ethiopia and North America, the recording sold 4.4 million albums by 16th May, 1985. Including T-shirts and 7.3 million singles, total estimated earnings from this song went well beyond the four million dollar mark.

Inspired by the success of Band Aid, Bob Geldof dreamed of a concert which would raise even more money in an attempt to solve some of Africa's most urgent problems such as their need for medicine and their unbelievable lack of irrigation. His dream eventually came true and on 13th July, 1985 two all-star benefit concerts were performed simultaneously, one at London's Wembley Stadium and the other at JFK Stadium in Philadelphia. This event, called Live Aid, had Phil Collins playing the drums with John Paul Jones, Jimmy Page, and Robert Plant. They appeared on the stage at 8 p.m. in Philadelphia to play three of their old Led Zeppelin songs.

Tickets for these concerts sold for a minimum of thirty-five dollars and the concerts were televised simultaneously in Great Britain and the United States. Donations also came via the telephone in England and America and all eventual proceeds came to over one hundred million dollars. All of my favourite performers played at these 1985 concerts: the rock group Queen at England's Wembley and also the extraordinary Elton John, Paul McCartney, and Pete Townshend. The event displayed new talents such as singer Sade, George Michael, U2 and Duran Duran and old ones like Bob Dylan, Keith Richards, Daryl Hall, John Oates, Ozzy Osbourne's Black Sabbath, David Crosby, Stephen Stills, Graham Nash, Neil Young, Mick Jagger and Tina Turner. Eric Clapton played 'Layla' and Elvis Costello played 'All You Need Is Love'.[3]

Elton John performs regularly at many charity events such as the Prince's Trust of 1986 and 1987, the Stand By Me AIDS benefit in 1987, Farm Aid IV in 1990, Knebworth 1990, A Concert For Life in 1992 and several Rainforest benefits such as those occurring in March of 1991 and 1992 at Carnegie Hall.[4]

On Monday nights I frequently listen to a live radio show called Rockline. On 7th April, 1997, drummer Jason Bonham, the son of late drummer, John Bonham, accompanied by a guitarist, a singer and a bass player played two hours of Led Zeppelin music. It was great fun and they played the tunes very well. They donated the profits from *In The Name Of My Father* and their tour to several of Jason Bonham's favourite charities.

In 1977 Page played in Sussex with Ron Wood to raise money for the Goaldiggers organisation which provides playgrounds for underprivileged children. Because an old acquaintance of his, Ronnie Lane, had multiple sclerosis, Jimmy Page played in an all-star benefit at Royal Albert Hall in London, England on 20th and 21st September, 1983. London's Royal Albert Hall seats six to eight thousand people. Sixty thousand dollars was raised for England's Action Research into Multiple Sclerosis (ARMS). These two performances included Eric Clapton, who joined Page and Jeff Beck to play 'Layla' and the events were attended by the Prince and Princess of Wales. The event also benefited The Prince's Trust, which supports self-help programmes for young people. Page played 'City Sirens', 'Who's to Blame' and 'Stairway to Heaven'. James Hooker played Albert Hall's pipe organ. Backstage, a Seiko, visual metronome which belonged to Jimmy Page was stolen[5].

Three months later, on 1st December, Page joined the ARMS benefit tour at the Cow Palace in San Francisco for three, consecutive, evening performances. The first night's set included an instrumental version of 'Stairway to Heaven' and a few other instrumental songs. By the third evening he played 'Boogie Woman' and other show-stoppers. These ARMS events also included guitarists Jeff Beck and Eric Clapton. The benefit tour also performed in Dallas, Texas, Los Angeles, California and ended at Madison Square Garden in New York for two nights.

Page played on Rolling Stone bassist, Bill Wyman's, album project: *Willie and The Poor Boys* of March of 1985 and Wyman donated his profits to Ronnie Lane's ARMS charity.

In England, at Knebworth, in June of 1990, the charity concert for the benefit of Nordoff-Robbins Music Therapy Centre entertained over one hundred thousand people. Robert Plant and Jimmy Page were two of the musical artists who performed and they played three Led Zeppelin songs. The event was shown on MTV and, of course I saw it. Jimmy Page looked splendid and he had white streaks running through the temples of his hair. The Nordoff-Robbins Music Therapy Centre uses music to treat mentally and physically challenged children. This event also raised money for the British Record Industry Trust School for Performing Arts and Technology. *Encomium: A Tribute to Led Zeppelin* was released in 1995, on which several bands played Led Zeppelin songs. Robert Plant and Tori Amos performed 'Down By the Seaside'. Sheryl Crow covered 'Dyer Maker', Stone Temple Pilots:

'Dancing Days', Duran Duran: 'Thank You', 4 Non Blondes: 'Misty Mountain Hop', Hootie & The Blowfish: 'Hey, Hey What Can I Do?', Cracker: 'Good Times, Bad Times', Rollins Band: 'Four Sticks', Never the Bride: 'Going to California', Big Head Todd & The Monsters: 'Tangerine', Blind Melon: 'Out on the Tiles', Helmet with David Yow: 'Custard Pie'.

Proceeds from this CD went to various children's charities. 7th December, 1997, saw Jimmy Page engaged in another performance for an English charity in which he and Robert Plant, Michael Lee, Charlie Jones played 'Over The Hills and Far Away' and 'Thank You'. In March 1998 Page donated fifteen thousand reais to a project called Graos de Luz, at the institute called Imas da Reparacao in Bahia, Brazil, which is a small, religious school for children near Lencois in Brazil.

From the 1995 Page–Plant North American tour, Miller Genuine Draft guaranteed one hundred thousand dollars to be raised for the Second Harvest, a food bank supply system for the United States.[6]

An organisation called Amnesty International works with governments to free political prisoners and to end political oppression. On December 10th December, 1998 performers Alanis Morrisette, Pete Gabriel, Tracy Chapman, Radiohead, Bruce Springsteen, and Jimmy Page and Robert Plant played their songs at the Palais Omni Sports Arena in Paris, Bercy-France to raise money for Amnesty related causes. The concert lasted from 6 p.m. until 1.40 a.m. and Jimmy Page and Robert Plant played second to last in the line-up.

Jimmy Page at the Messezentrum Halle A, Nürnberg, Germany, 27th June 1980.
Photograph courtesy of Richard Falzone.

Cultural Curves

The English never draw a line without blurring it.
                                        Winston Churchill

The Gibson brand of electric guitar is perfect for producing a weighty sound and Jimmy Page most frequently plays guitars made by the Gibson company. His rock music is either loud, dark, heavy or ethereal and by being so moody, in a purposeful way, stakes claim to the Romantic music form of the nineteenth century. In its individualism lie both the profound mystery of darkness and an intensely clear honesty. The human love of music goes far back to the Greeks of 500 BC and the East Indians of 1500 BC.

Much modern music, in general, by my perception, has went the way of the 1950s, with the sanitised and contrived appearances of singers and the bland, heavily engineered sounds I usually hear on top forty radio stations. One hard rock station consoles its listeners by playing an enormous percentage of songs which were recorded in the 1970s. There are many new genres of music now. One of the most lucrative seems to be the Latin, whose songs are called romantic ballads, when they are really only lyrical manifestos of emotional misery with no resolve. The singers of these songs are usually of the most beautiful and attractive people on earth. Let me stress here, that music production has become a very crowded room. Page's former musical partner, Paul Rodgers, has an album called

Now and the track 'Soul of Love' clocks in at number sixteen, on one of *Billboard* magazine's many charts, this week of 13th September, 1997.

The most impressive rock band to carry the Romance of heavy metal music into the 1990s was called the Cult. *Love*, released in 1985, contains interesting and energetic music. Vocalist Ian Astbury is intensely physical in his singing performances and he is strikingly beautiful to look at with huge, black eyes and hair like black satin. His voice is pure, clear and very strong. The music of Love carries me to a spiritual dimension where I feel most comfortable. Some song titles here are 'Nirvana', 'The Phoenix' and 'Black Angel'. Guitar sounds are mixed to achieve deep and hollow sounds. The release from their debut album of 1984 was called *Spirit Walker*. The Cult has a relatively small body of work as does Led Zeppelin. Quality is not determined by numbers of released recordings. Output thus far by the Cult is as follows: *Dreamtime* (1983), *Love* (1985), *Electric*, *Sonic Temple*, *Sonic Temple Hologram*, *Ceremony* (1991), Love mixes, and the Manner sessions.

These musicians are not, and do not aspire to be the beautiful elite as is Jimmy Page. Astbury and guitarist Billy Duffy are a hungrier, yet earthier breed of artist, not so elegant, of which type resembles the hippy poets of the 1960s in their anti-materialism. These artists make their statement subliminally rather than conspicuously.

Song titles on *Ceremony* are: 'Ceremony', 'Wild Hearted Son', 'Earth Mofo', 'White', 'If', 'Full Tilt', Heart of Soul', 'Bangkok Rain', 'Indian', 'Sweet Salvation' and 'Wonderland'.

All elements of Romanticism are present in this work along with graphic nature descriptions such as crystal snow and winds of change. Earth is worthy of important emphasis to these individuals. They wonder in a childlike way about surviving industrialisation. They want nothing except to live creatively. There is little arrogance here and purity of purpose is obvious on the CD cover which bears the face of a beautiful, dark-haired child.

Led Zeppelin's final concert performance took place on 7th July, 1980. When drummer, John Bonham died in September of 1980, Led Zeppelin was finished thus leaving a heavy metal vacancy. Many were called and it seemed all were, eventually, chosen to fill the void: Def Leppard, Dokken, Guns and Roses, Iron Maiden, Queensryche, Whitesnake and many more all vied for the heavy metal crown and while doing so earned many fans and millions of dollars. Even though I was very busy during this decade and did not purchase much of this music, I was persistently disturbed by the presence of a peculiarly ordinary sounding rock music being played on the radio.

By 1985 American art, music and advertising began to reflect an emphasis on anxiety and loneliness rather than the luxury of surrealism. The work of British rock band Pink Floyd is as disturbing as a Picasso painting. Sense of the presence of the gigantic landscape and wishing for transcendent experience and timeless subject matter were being replaced by the tragic. The energetic precision, beauty and sublimity present in Presence became more and more difficult to find in new music. Paranoia is absent from the work of Led Zeppelin and their works are usually interesting.

On 1st August, 1981 MTV (a twenty-four hour music channel) became available to paying cable subscribers, thus fully commercialising music. This commercial victory of the Warner Brothers conglomerate was followed by the availability of compact discs which offered clearer sound than vinyl records. MTV led to the look of musicians being emphasised as much and oftentimes more than the sound. It is uncanny that Led Zeppelin's *Coda* was released in early 1982 because the entire catalogue of their music was completed just under the wire of the beginning of a rash of lesser music being performed publicly solely for its visual marketability. In other words artists began to feel they had to look good on MTV before they could sell their music. After ten years of being bombarded with mad-cap and glossified music videos many people suddenly began to truly appreciate great music again.

In the 1990s there arrived an aesthetic of sorts in that lyrical emphasis had truly expanded to encompass a huge variety of outlooks and human emotions. Led Zeppelin imagination was big and this marked their music as Romantic. On the Page–Plant production *No Quarter* the new songs move vividly through the Romantic. Plant and Page created a lengthy video for MTV and called it *Unledded* which is comprised of songs from their *No Quarter* CD. A friend of Jimmy Page made a tape of North African drum loops and this began his work on the project. The songs on *No Quarter* are of a world type of music; some of which were recorded in Morocco and Marrakech, they contain mid-Eastern flair. The importance of world issues to Page and Plant made it imperative for them to broaden their gentle, yet robustly, Romantic song lyrics. The importance of the heavy metal genre of music will always be maintained as long as it aids us in the understanding of human frailties. Plant and Page have a keen appreciation for the different types of music available and they are thus able to create with diversity which gives outstanding quality to their work.

In October of 1994, MTV aired the video starring Jimmy Page and Robert Plant and many expert musicians, *Unledded* begins with the two stars singing and playing music in the woods. During breaks Page is captured smoking cigarettes to keep himself quiet. The first stage shot is a deep purple colour and they play a sparkling, new version of 'Thank You'. The beautiful love of Robert Plant named Nadjma Akhtar joins him on vocals while the mandolin plays 'The Battle of Evermore'. My favourite, 'Gallows Pole' is a fabulous dance music, and the original song dates back to 1692 from England. The viewer journeys back to the natural beauty of Wales for 'Nobody's Fault But Mine' where Robert Plant sings on a rocky mountain side with Charlie Jones playing a stand-up bass, Nigel Eaton his hurdy-gurdy, ex-guitar player from the Cure, Porl Thompson plays a banjo and Jimmy Page a double Ovation.

There is a cute dog wandering around the players at the beginning of the video. Work on the *No Quarter* project commenced at London's King's Cross in early 1994.

In front of hundreds of people in Marrakech, Morocco Jimmy Page wears all white and the song 'Yallah' shows him making strange, spaceship noises with his theremin and his 1959 electric, Gibson Sunburst. The songs 'Yallah', 'City Don't Cry' and 'Wah Wah' were all created by Page and Plant while in Marrakech. Page plays an acoustic with four local musicians (known as Gnaoua) sitting on a blanket in the courtyard of what appears to be a very old building. The Gnaoua were once slaves of African descent who were brought, forcefully, to Morocco by Arabs. Their special musical sounds provide an important, healing, social function in Marrakech. This is a pretty and colourful video which includes a different guitar in each song. It raises my blood pressure and makes my heart beat quicker to see Page in performance. Ed Shearmur plays a Hammond organ, Jim Sutherland a mandolin and Michael Lee, the drums in the concert portions of this video. The video display of the song 'No Quarter' shows Page playing his twelve-string and in 'Thank You' he stands playing his Sunburst. The acoustic portion of the song 'No Quarter' was filmed at Delgath Falls in England and other portions were recorded at a slate quarry in a British town called

Corris. For 'The Battle of Evermore' the guitar he plays has three fretboards and nothing but good feelings emanate from the song 'That's The Way'. The musicians here are all interesting and beautiful in their own unique way.

Members of the London Metropolitan Orchestra perform in several songs. These are twenty-nine pieces of violins, violas and cellos played by highly skilled string players and the performance is overwhelming because of the quality of the music.

Seeing Page and Plant in this video was great for people of my generation because most of us missed their tours of the 1970s, but we all heard their music on the radio. The video definitely shows the viewer who they are and the simultaneous release of the CD *No Quarter* gave new listeners a chance to be fans of Led Zeppelin, but with expanded versions of seven of their earlier songs. Some of which are barely recognisable through the change. Others like 'Since I've Been Loving You' have become excruciatingly moving. Page's twenty-four years of perfecting and streamlining the notes of this song has made this the greatest blues song of all time. The *Unledded* video and *No Quarter* CD promoted their then upcoming world tour. In the 20th April, 1995 issue of *Rolling Stone* is to be found an article describing their sixth date, in Miami. Here, Parke Puterbaugh describes Page as 'blindingly brilliant' and says he performed as a man unleashed. The 1995 Page–Plant American tour began on 26th February, 1995, the European part of their world tour began in June and the entire tour grossed thirty-five million dollars.

I had the opportunity to see Jimmy Page and Robert Plant on 12th May, 1995, the date of my graduation from UNLV, and I attended the concert at the MGM Grand Garden with my two best friends instead of my own graduation ceremony. A band called the Tragically Hip opened and played for an outrageously long time, but when the Hip finally finished their set the concert was about as much fun as I have ever had. I danced and sang during the entire event. To say I became mystified with the music of Jimmy Page would be to grossly understate the emotion his music elicits and the universal appeal it is known to have. A group of eight Egyptian string players, called the Egyptian Pharaohs, and some Las Vegas string players joined them for the last hour of the show during which they performed 'Kashmir' before a delighted thirteen thousand fans. I loved their version of the Doors' 'Break on Through (to the other side)'. Everyone on the ground floor jumped and danced all the way through the concert's melodies, some of which were 'Black Dog', 'In The Evening' and 'Shake My Tree'. They were spectacular. Robert Plant wriggled around and Jimmy Page played his many different guitars while wearing a blue silk blouse and a small, gold cross around his neck. I have never seen anyone as strong as Robert Plant before; I just kept wishing he would not have stood in front of Jimmy Page so much.

In May of 1995 I took what I saw to be a gift of the universe (the simultaneous coincidence of my graduation from UNLV with a Bachelor of Arts degree in English and the date of their concert) and turned it into this book about the best of music during my lifetime. Following this May show, on 13th May, the band played the San Diego sports arena. 16th and 17th May dates marked attendance of 32,429 people at the Great Western Forum in Inglewood, California, 19th May, Page and Plant played in Oakland, California, and on 26th May in Vancouver, British Columbia.

The reasons the music of Jimmy Page can be classified as Romantic are many, but I go even further than this in stating his music markedly extends the Romantic era. No other hard rock music displays the splendorous lyrics and thrilling music in such a Romantic format. Shelley, Keats and Byron would be proud of Jimmy Page.

Over a third of Led Zeppelin music was played on an acoustic rather than an electric guitar and in these instances Page managed to pull a lucent and heavy metal sound out of his six and twelve stringed acoustic guitars. With his banjos and mandolins he brought folk music into the rock world. One would be hard pressed in 1997 to see a heavy-metal guitarist playing any acoustic instruments. I have not, with the exception of the Page–Plant shows. Having been born and raised in Las Vegas, the kingdom of popular culture, I have grown to truly appreciate Jimmy Page for being the only reigning rock musician who has never regurgitated popular culture back into my face. His rock music always contains an other worldliness often referring to love and comes from an ancient and eternal place in the sunlit dusk of evening.

On the last Saturday of August in 1995, shortly after noon, my little dog, Cherry, brought me a Reno, Nevada newspaper. The front page told of Jimmy Page–Robert Plant tickets going on sale at 1 p.m. for a 6th October concert to be held in Sacramento, California at the Cal expo. When I purchased my tickets, I found out about another 7th October, Saturday night concert which would be in Mountain View, California. I purchased tickets and would attend both shows. A band called Blind Melon opened these two shows. At 9.27 p.m. on 6th October, Robert Plant announced to the crowd that he had known Jimmy Page for twenty-seven years, he then declared the Egyptian Pharaohs to be the finest musicians available. The songs they played this night were organised the same way as the MGM Grand Garden show I had seen in May except for Page and his musicians played an overly lengthened 'Whole Lotta Love', which this crowd psychically demanded.

The 7th October, Mountain View concert was held at Bill Graham's Shoreline, an outdoor arena where I stood five feet in front of Jimmy Page during the concert. There was the presence of a huge white candle, four feet wide and six feet tall, burning on the right side of the stage before the show began and all throughout the show. This concert differed from the two previous shows I had seen in two very important ways: before the show began, I witnessed James Patrick Page standing alone in the dark, inhaling cigarette smoke deeply for at least four minutes. Later, when he was seated with one of his guitars, the flirt smiled at me. The beautiful girlfriend of Robert Plant, Nadjma Akhtar, appeared here to sing 'The Battle of Evermore with Robert Plant. She wore a turquoise sari studded with gold stars and she added a deep and feminine grace to the full mooned night. The song 'Whole Lotta Love' on this night included 'How Many More Times', 'We're Gonna Groove', 'Break on Through' and 'Dazed and Confused'. The 1995 Page–Plant tour allowed taping and this particular concert produced a bootlegged recording of the event.

I could not let the glimpse I had of this blithe man go to waste. There is much to be said about all influential artists, but I chose James Patrick Page to base a novel on because of the influence his music has had on me and my entire generation of rock concert attendees. My little newspaper retriever has never delivered another newspaper to me.

The feelings elicited by good music are rarely superficial even though musicians may have superficial reasons for wanting to become performers. Certainly, popular musicians love the applause at the end of a song, set or show and most celebrities like having the attention of large groups of people. Personally, I admire a shy person, such as Jimmy Page, who is able to overcome a stage fright to display his various movements, his fascinating music and his mystifying, male, rock star smile. I have heard men say they do not really care what women think of them. If this were generally true the human race would be in danger of extinction. This type of comment is most often made by men who have been rejected by a woman. However, these type of comments are becoming outdated and we as a civilisation of people are moving forward. As confused as our sex roles may appear, we all seem to want to be treated equally and fairly.

I will never forget Jimmy Page and his adorable, childlike smile. I bet he has broken many a heart with that charming smile. As the huge candles burned and the hair of Robert Plant shone like a yellow silk as bright as the Egyptian sun draped luxuriously over his dark clothing, I left the arena as 'Kashmir' rang out over the city. Nature filled my solitude with love and beauty on this night. The stars shone brightly and California introduced its glamour to me as I headed for the beach shore. I was extended an invitation, by one of the Egyptian Pharaohs, to meet Sir Page at the Fairmount Hotel in San Francisco. As I stood waiting for my taxi, which he insisted was not going to appear, the creepy violin player kept putting his arm around my shoulder. I have never understood men who, before they know your first name, are treating you like a bed partner. I did not go in search of Page with the Pharaoh. I headed back home to Nevada to write this book. Somehow I knew if Merlin could transport Stonehenge from Ireland, I could make the magic of a Jimmy Page concert understandable to future generations.

On 21st November, 1995, Peter Grant, Led Zeppelin's wonderful manager during the 1970s, died of a heart attack at age sixty. He played an essential role in the group's enormous success.

Led Zeppelin were voted into the Rock and Roll Hall of Fame at a dinner at the Waldorf Astoria Hotel in New York

City on 12th January, 1995. Four days later (on a full moon) Sir Page loves to do important things on the occasion of a full moon, Jimmy Page divorced Patricia Ecker and left her six million dollars so as to take care of their son.[1]

There is much interest in the Page–Plant combination. The contrast between their visual appearances is attractive; the bouncy, blond Plant with the usually stationary, dark-haired Black Irish look of Jimmy Page. Contrary to appearances, Page is extroverted and Plant introverted. Both are British, and this heritage endowed the two with the wisdom to create brilliant Romantic music. They share a fondness for Druidic lore, magic and all things transcendentally beautiful. The magical Merlin built Stonehenge, a place most beloved by Jimmy Page.

The Druids were mediators between earthly life and the eternal world. They were also looked on by the Celtic peoples of Ireland, England and Wales to make important judgements in civil situations. God places a great deal of value on judgement, it is written so in the Holy Bible. The Danube River in Germany is named after the Druidic Mother goddess Danus.[2] The Druids formed their cult during the first millennium and only a fortunate few have held on to their wisdom until this day. Winston Churchill installed himself into the Albion Lodge division of the Druids in 1908. The name of the current Page–Plant music publishing company is Flame of Albion Music.

Women love music, we love to sing, dance, write songs and pound on drums. We play flutes and compose lullabies in our sacred groves. Women worship nature and generally do these things for free. Music has always been a magical way to achieve a spiritual state of mind. The rhythms of nature today can still be found in the natural landscape, but these rhythms are also anxiously sought in music. Music which reaches deeply into our hearts and souls is what women love to hear. Musical talent is, at least partially, dependent on the intelligent demand of music lovers and more women attend concerts than men.

Both Page and Plant are antiquated in their thinking and by reaching back hundreds of years for their musical inspirations they appear progressive on the 1994 CD *No Quarter*. On the song 'Yallah' Page and Plant went for the Moroccan trance type of music. In the 1970s, writer William Burroughs likened Led Zeppelin music to the Moroccan trance music of the Jajouka tribe. In the song reality is taken away from the listener. These tribes in Morocco delight in a trance music which they consider curative. This music sometimes consists of monotonous tones which are capable of producing a trance. The music of the Jajouka often consists of one to five drummers and the drums are usually hand drums. Other instruments include pipes, horns, flutes, and the rhaita. The song 'Wonderful One' is proof that mankind is capable of pure love.

Until the Moroccan and folk influences, the only traditional music upon which Page relied in the creation of his music was the blues. His artistic fulfilment comes through following a path of self-discovery rather than one of self-aggrandisement. It is a disciplined path which has enabled him to find God in his own way. His discriminate use of intuition and instinct are what give him an intimate connection with his fans. This non-conforming type of self-expression is never painless, but he made it look as effortless on stage in front of fifty-six thousand eight hundred people in Tampa, Florida on 5th May, 1973 as he did twenty-two years later when I saw him.

Page makes more of a statement here about the state of world affairs simply by acknowledging the world than he would if he were to go into a political foray and scream about what is wrong. Violence is a part of our world. Part of the appeal of alternative music is that its startling power and high volume are violent sounding. Darkness and ignorance are embraced by made-up glamour bands who after they have squeezed millions of dollars out of bored teenagers and then perform publicly only for fun, can afford them. If we lived in a reasonable world full of reasonable people all music would probably be uplifting and pleasant to hear. However, we live in a world of close to six billion people, each of which, apparently, has a different opinion. Consequently, there are few of these who contribute positive and fun sound vibrations to the atmosphere. This is why I offer my humble obeisances to the few musicians of my lifetime whose music has made me feel good.

The warm, friendly voice of Robert Plant lends much to the appeal of the *No Quarter* CD. The skill of the Egyptian Ensemble is admirable and truly, stellar musicianship is displayed by all of the musicians who participated here. They are playing music which uplifts and illuminates the universe just as stars brighten up the dark sky. This intelligent band knows that as modern musicians they yield power to entertain, but they use their musical medium to enlighten and uplift the audience as well. Robert Plant is no slouch in the intellect department and he speaks Arabic quite well, I am told.

Page and Plant think music should flow evenly and pleasurably. Much of the mystery in their music comes from the imaginative world they have exploited in their music. This world is non-violent and aesthetically pleasing. No Quarter is a collection of music that carries the mystery of Egypt and Morocco. This music, until Page and Plant, had been most notably mastered by the Master musicians of the Jajouka tribe. Now one only needs to go to this CD to experience the music of the hills of the Jebel in Tangier or the hot Moroccan sun in 'Kashmir'. Guitarist Brian

Jones and authors William Burroughs and Brion Gysin journeyed to these places to understand the music long before Page and Plant.

This music is the classical music of the Andalusian court of Seville, Spain of the ninth and tenth centuries. Madrid, Spain, a place I know and love, is where my grandparents were born and is one thousand kilometres north of Fez, Morocco. In 1492 those roving court musicians were ousted with the Moors from the South of Spain and they drifted around playing their music. The Moroccans consider the music, which Page and Plant display to perfection on this CD, their national music.[3]

Page and Plant spared no expense in making this music authentic. Bendir and finger cymbals are played by Khaliq, one of the players in the Egyptian ensemble. The Grove Dictionary defines this instrument this way:

> A bendir is a circular single headed drum related to the Islamic duff. It is found in Islamic North Africa; the term probably derives from a Spanish word applied to an Arab frame drum in Muslim, Spain. It is a large tambourine with two snares, known mainly among the Berbers of Algeria and Morocco.

Cymbals originated in India. To play five pairs of small cymbals is regarded by many as mystical. The CD is an extreme effort by Page and Plant to display their own wisdom and their mystical world to their audience. Within the Egyptian ensemble of eleven players there are two duf players, two bendir players, a Reque instrumentalist, four string players, a flautist who plays an Egyptian bamboo flute and Kheir who plays an Oud. The duff has specific associations with certain places, but is a term given to a single headed frame drum. Robert Plant's vocals are outstanding on every song. What I most remember about the Page–Plant 1995 show was the performers were devoted to giving their music to the audience in their most professional manner and the shows I attended contained two English gentlemen trying very hard to preserve and display the musical brotherhood of the Gnaoua who play a variety of instruments. I liked that.

Cadence

To say the word Romanticism is to say modern art, that is intimacy, spirituality, colour, aspiration towards the infinite, expressed by every means available to the arts.

Charles Baudelaire

My dictionary defined the blues in 1807. This definition begins with the words blue devils in brackets. Defined first as low spirits and melancholy and second like this: 'a song of lamentation characterised by usu. 12-bar phrases, 3-line stanzas in which the words of the second line usu. repeat those of the first and continual occurrence of blue notes in melody and harmony.'[1]

I describe the blues as living in poverty without someone to love.

In the 1930s Dallas, Texas was one of many blues meccas in the United States. Black skinned guitarists with names such as T-Bone Walker, Blind Willie Johnson and Blind Lemon Jefferson played guitar in nightclubs for tip money. Guitarist Huddie (Leadbelly) Leadbetter toured nightclubs, but spent most of his time trying to get out of jail. Leadbelly was the first American singer to record the old English folk song, 'Gallis Pole'.

A man named John Lomax researched American music by driving all over America making field recordings. His son, Allen, became a renowned musicologist after he made a field recording of the blues guitarist Muddy Waters in

1941. Allen Lomax drove all over the United States of America during the 1940s and 1950s, listening and recording many of our musical artists.[2]

Being on the road playing the blues has always been an arduous way to earn a living. I have described some ways in which the music of Jimmy Page has maintained the realm of high culture. He has shared a distaste for listening to or creating a popular culture type of music, with other virtuoso guitarists such as the late Stevie Ray Vaughan who in spite of dying young left a lasting impression on the music we call the blues. These are merely observations, however, I know that the appeal of great blues and Romantic hard rock music, for me, is its uncanny ability to offer an out of body and surreal experience. I always explain anything which accomplishes this as being spiritually profound. I find audio, sensual experiences useful in furthering my spiritual life while enhancing my physical one.

I am not going to waste paper advocating or criticising a music played by angry teenagers any more than I would use this format to express popular, feminist frustrations because I prefer to dwell on things which bring us together as human beings. I believe blues music is one of the most wonderful of these things. Maybe someday there will be legions of young women guitarists with the ability to play powerful blues songs, however, now is the time I am addressing and today that is simply not the scenario on display. There are a few, talented female, guitarists around: Lucinda Williams, Bonnie Raitt, and Lita Ford, but the majority of recorded electric, guitar music seems to be played by the male sex of our species. I do not begrudge men credit for playing guitar well.

In my lifetime jazz music has been a wonderful combination of the emotion of blues music and the polish, sophistication and restraint that is exhibited by well practised musicians. I associate jazz music with the city of New Orleans. However, literature which discusses music can suffer when it must quantify all music as being of a specific genre. I know my use of the term heavy metal to describe part of the canon of music created by Page alienates many while it fascinates some of my readers. I may as well state here precisely what I mean by it. I use the word heavy to insinuate meaningful and profound and metal to relate to electric, guitar string sounds. At this the genre suddenly expands, does it not? Robert Plant has called the song 'How Many More Times' psychedelic jazz.

Blues music is softly expressive. Manic depression created an impressive female, Romantic blues singer named, Billie Holiday, who had a clean and strong type of beauty. Her voice was sincere, rich and warm. She wanted to have class and she achieved a superior type of this through her work. In her voice was reflected a childlike expression of love, an innocent search for love, and a bold willingness to give that love in her own way. Lasting favourites sung by her are 'God Bless the Child', and 'T'Aint Nobody's Business If I Do'. Billie Holiday performed these songs at the Sahara Hotel in 1958. Billie Holiday epitomised the American jazzy blues singer until 1959.

In 1972 Robert Plant and Jimmy Page met Elvis Presley in his International Hotel suite in Las Vegas, Nevada. It was only natural that Page would want to meet Presley, the most famous entertainer in history. It is hard to imagine them having much to talk about, but I am sure the meeting was delightful for all. In 1969, when Led Zeppelin was beginning its rise to fame, Elvis Presley was entertaining nightly in the International Hotel showroom. On these nights he would sing selections from his abundant repertoire of hit songs, songs such as 'Kentucky Rain', 'Suspicious Minds', 'Burning Love' and 'If I Can Dream' which was originally recorded at American Sound Studios in Memphis, Tennessee.

Elvis Presley was born nine years and one day earlier than Jimmy Page on 8th January, 1935 in Tupelo, Mississippi. In 1946, Elvis Aaron Presley began to play guitar. Like the career of Page, Presley's career was set in motion by astute management skills. There was a major difference between the way the two stars were handled though. Jimmy Page was never 'handled'; he called all the shots. Elvis Presley was viewed by MGM movie studios, RCA recording, and the Presley manager, Colonel Tom Parker, as a money machine. During his short lifetime of forty-two years, Elvis Presley made more than thirty films, all in which he was the leading star, and at least twenty-five recordings. I attended one of the many performances Elvis Presley gave at the International Hotel. My privileged attendance came in 1972, a night in which his music touched my heart very deeply. Elvis sang 'In The Ghetto' and 'Amazing Grace' along with many more of his hit songs. He played the piano and the dramatic, yet, down to earth, way he presented himself on the stage was adorable. His voice was warm, unique and emotional as he sang gospel songs that elicited powerful, emotional responses from every member. No one who ever saw Elvis Presley in concert will ever forget him as the King. Elvis Presley died in 1977 as Led Zeppelin delved into their final world tour.

In 1962 Atlantic Records had acquired all of the old, Memphis-Stax master recordings. In 1969 when Led Zeppelin delivered their first two albums via the Atlantic label, executives Ahmet Ertegun and Jerry Wexler had already signed Cream including Eric Clapton to their ATCO subsidiary. This meaning that the Atlantic label managed to acquire, even if only temporarily, both of the greatest, white, blues guitarists of the twentieth century and most of the early, American, rhythm and blues music as performed by its original, African–American pioneers. Who says businessmen do not know good music when they hear it?[3]

Robert Plant is a most thrilling, blues singer because of the extreme energy which he gives to his performance. The strengths of Page have been in his stubborn perseverance at achieving a superior sound and he has always attacked the blues with this type of endurance. When Page is assisted by vocalists such as Robert Plant or David Coverdale, who with a painstaking perfection make the audience feel the bliss of happiness or the pain of abandonment, their soulful performances are unbeatable. Hard, rock music which includes old songs, and 1940s, Memphis Minnie style combined with guitar artistry and passionate singing is what Page and Plant deliver and is what makes their fans so devoted to them.

Singing and playing the blues is a distinctive, creative outlet and it has enabled many inspired souls to become all they are capable of and blues music can be inspirational to those who hear it. Fleetwood Mac was a superlative blues band before Stevie Nicks joined them as a balladeer, then they became a popular, rock band. Ms Nicks sang and wrote a few songs which laid emphasis on a Welsh witch, a gold dust woman, a gypsy and a few visions here and there.[4] I always found it remarkable that blatant accusations upon her or Fleetwood Mac of being Satan worshipers were non-existent in print. The latter incarnation of Fleetwood Mac touted lyrics which referred to women as witches, cocaine use and psychic visions for their Romantic elements. The Romantic rock ballads of Jimmy Page had song titles such as 'Dancing Days', 'The Ocean' and 'Stairway to Heaven'! The point here is that in the five year space between the dawn of Led Zeppelin music and the entrance of Ms Nicks upon the music scene, the occult mystery theme had become so pervasive in rock music that the subject no longer received attention in the press.

In the catalogue of Led Zeppelin music there are allusions referent to Satan. One of these is found on *Physical Graffiti* in the song 'The Houses of the Holy'. The lyric goes: 'From the houses of the holy, we can watch the white doves go / From the dark of Satan's door, and it only goes to show, you know'.

These lyrics are clumsy and do not say as much as they pretend to. It is obvious to me that Page and Plant are using the S word because they know it will get attention and they long to present themselves as mystical and deep. On 'Achilles Last Stand' from Presence Plant sings: 'The devil's in his hole.' On 'No Quarter': 'the devil mocks their every step' and on 'Nobody's Fault But Mine', 'The devil told me to roll'. Ooh, scary!

Sometimes I grow so tired of books written by Ivy League graduates in which my favourite musicians are simplistically labelled as misogynists or devil worshipers. What comes to mind as a result of my exposure to this type of literature is a surety that the writer never listened to the music and was overly reliant upon rumours heard. I am left thinking that Ivy League Universities probably do not dispel knowledge of rock musicians or their music and that the required reading lists are so enormous the students have no time left to listen to music. I really enjoy literature written by people who listen to the music before they write about it.

According to *Guitar Player* magazine and numerous other sources, there had been a minority twenty year tradition of listening to Negro popular music in Britain by 1944, the year of Jimmy Page's birth.[5] Of all the earliest Negro blues guitarists, Muddy Waters, seems to have been the most relevant to Eric Clapton, Jimmy Page and Keith Richards, who all refer to him as an influence. Eric Clapton, who is the most adamantly purist of the three, will play nothing which he does not consider blues,

Richards rarely strays from the rhythm and blues sound and Page goes in whatever direction his heart and expertise take him. In fact he considers the blues portal as something he has walked through to get to where he is today as an artist. While Americans, largely, ignored the early, American, blues guitarists these English musicians did not.

I am not blind to the shortcomings of the personalities of rock stars nor am I ignorant of the decadence of some rock music. I am not a chronic Anglophile. However, I am elitist in my ideas about the superiority of the body of music created by Jimmy Page. I see it as a pearl in a string of pearls, a foundational standard upon which much glorious and beautiful music will be built in the future. For those of us who are into that.

After we have enjoyed and, if desirable, understood the origins of the music, the language is how we are left to perceive the music of Jimmy Page. Though an attempt was made, on his fourth LP, with the four respective symbols, to complicate or perhaps enlarge the message, the lyrics are extremely simple and refined. One technique rarely exhibited in these lyrics is that of repetition. I appreciate this because nothing bores me quicker than monotonously redundant lyrics. These lyrics are euphonious, but the songwriters did not feel a strong need to rhyme, subsequently the songs say exactly what the writers meant. Interestingly, the songs make no reference to the British monarchy, downtown streets, or other locales familiar to them, only rare, pastoral references are made to their native England. Some of their later works draw their inspiration from places outside of their homeland.

On 'Dazed and Confused' the lyrics question the present bed mate: 'Will your tongue wag so much, when I send you to hell?'

It is sad, but true, ladies, here once again, are the Page–Plant duo macho posturing, and threatening. It is unfortunate that the two ended up being misogynists but these lyrics make it obvious that the successful Robert Plant and Jimmy Page became arrogant men who disrespected women and not having the political savvy of the punks who would follow them, directed their anger at the opposite sex as is so often done by some men.

There is a lack of pageantry in Led Zeppelin music, which is simply the living of life in musical conversation. Even 'Stairway to Heaven', a song about a lady, is a simple story which wants those who hear it to reach toward their highest aspirations. Robert Plant wrote the lyrics to this song and he credits a book by Lewis Spence, the *Magic Arts in Celtic Britain*, as inspiration.[6]

There once was a roving guitar and harmonica playing singer named Robert Johnson, who born black and poor, in Hazelhurst, Mississippi, was expected to work in cotton fields. He decided in the 1920s he did not want to work there so he travelled around and played in St Louis nightclubs. Inspired by Son House, he developed a blues playing guitar style that people responded to rather affectionately. In November of 1936 he recorded a few of his songs in San Antonio, Texas. In June of the following year he recorded ten more songs in Dallas, Texas. One of these songs was 'Travelling Riverside Blues'. For whatever reason, most likely a desire to replicate a blues feeling in their music, thirty-two years later, Plant and Page lifted the following idea from Johnson's song: 'Squeeze my lemon 'til the juice run down my leg'.[7]

A similar lyric can be found on 'The Lemon Song' on *Led Zeppelin II* and states: 'squeeze me baby 'til the juice runs down my leg, the way you squeeze my lemon, I'm going to fall right out of bed.'

The pair also borrowed Johnson's title: 'Hellhound on My Trail' for a lyrical passage in their song 'The Ocean' and the lyric 'I have a bird that whistles' in 'You Shook Me' came from Johnson's 'Stones in My Passway'.

Huddy Leadbetter first recorded 'Gallis Pole' in 1939. The Page and Plant song, 'Gallows Pole' which they borrowed from this oral blues tradition is similar to the earlier recording, but is infinitely superior to it.

A popular critical viewpoint blames rock music for a decay in the modern morals belonging to the youth of today. The music has been said to elicit sexual feelings. This is somehow seen, by some, as a negative. Young people like to have sex. I think musical entertainments which display wild, sexual desires are beneficial because these, like any of the natural human creative urges, are better discussed honestly than thwarted in young people. Adolph Hitler was a thwarted and frustrated artist. Some thinkers are concerned about rock music because it is enjoyed by young people who have extraordinarily impressionable minds. I say the sooner we learn to discriminate upon the things we prefer as individuals the better.

One critic, Allan Bloom, is concerned that the music of Mick Jagger is detrimental and he states: 'I believe it ruins the imagination of young people and makes it very difficult for them to have a passionate relationship to the art and thought that are the substance of liberal education.'[8]

Thankfully Allan Bloom addresses more consequential matters than listening to rock music, but to his argument I can only particulate: when listening to music replaces concentration and study, a ruined imagination is a definite possibility and obsessing over rock music, as I do, might tend to narrow one's viewpoint. However, in my particular educational situation my passions about modern music filled an archaic and sterile void that was the main portion of my 'liberal' education. Bloom's viewpoint is a tired belief that has been directed, by various critics over the years, at any music which becomes trendy. Newspaper writers labelled ragtime as vulgar in the 1920s. The same was said of jazz music which began in New Orleans in the 1920s, by 1940 jazz music flourished and turned into swing, and by the mid 1950s had developed into rhythm and blues which is played best in the latter part of this millennium by a group of British oldsters who have called themselves the Rolling Stones since 1965, but as everyone knows the creamiest and most celestial blues player of them all is Eric Clapton. His 1998 offering *Pilgrim* shows him to have polished the raw texture of his blues guitar artistry to fit a 1990s format.

Content and Style

I feel that some so-called progressive groups have gone too far with their personalised intellectualism of beat music. Our music is essentially emotional like the old, rock stars of the past... We are not going to make any political or moral statements. Our music is simply us.

Jimmy Page

In 1998 Page and the newly popular rap artist, Puff Daddy, remade the wondrous 'Kashmir' into a song called 'Come With Me' for the soundtrack to the film *Godzilla* which landed in cinemas on 23rd May, of 1998. On 9th May, 1998, the two performed the song on the NBC television show, Saturday Night Live. This is one of the ways in which Page constantly expands his reach by keeping an open mind about his music. What I find so inspiring about the new music he has made is that it has exceeded my expectations so completely. This particular performance was vivacious and I do not remember ever seeing Page so animated. He is never afraid of giving his audience a taste of his music before it becomes available commercially.

During the 1998 Page–Plant tour Jimmy Page began most of his shows playing one of three Gibson Sunburst guitars during the first four songs. On this tour, he worked three of these through his show: his number one 1958 Gibson Sunburst, his number two 1959 Gibson Sunburst, a number three duplicate of the 1958 which he had made.

A Gibson 6/12 stringed double neck is used when he plays 'Tangerine' and 'Gallows Pole'. A red and black, electric, Sitar brand by Jerry James guitars, and a blue, Parker brand Nitefly which glowed maroon at times during the show were both used intermittently throughout shows. He used a theremin and a wah-wah pedal during those performances. The theremin, to me, is a complicated instrument. It is an electronic box which, with the interaction of human hands, controls the pitch and volume of sounds. Page always has it on his stage and during performances he steps over to it, once or twice, and waves his hands around the top of it.

Most heavy metal music of the 1990s has been neatly tucked under the label of alternative music. At first, as is often the case with musical genres, this music as played by groups Soundgarden, Nirvana, Pearl Jam and Alice in Chains was spectacular. For its grungy, metal feel and relevant statement it came in as a breath of fresh air. The music of Pearl Jam warranted the attention of Page and Plant in 1998 in that the two attempted litigation in court over an alleged similarity between the Pearl Jam song 'Given to Fly' and the old Led Zeppelin song 'Going To California'.

The age in which we live necessitates art forms which are meaningful. Modern alternative music is important, it asks questions which need answers and it looks reality in the face. There are certain sociological perspectives about why famous, rock groups of the 1970s produced such a non-political flavour of lyric in favour of one which referred to sex and escape. Some say audiences were easy to manipulate during the period because most smoked pot, which is certainly a valid argument. All I can offer now is the assurance that the male, chauvinistic crap that Led Zeppelin dished out, and was swallowed up, so readily, by fans in the 1970s has been banished from the Page–Plant repertoire of the 1990s. I would like to think that Page and Plant have a bit more respect for women now, but I know that the two suddenly developing a respect for women is about as likely as me becoming President of the United States of America. However, the two have had enough savvy to exclude the song lyrics of 'Living Loving Maid', 'She's just a woman' from their 1990s song and dance routine. Although that lyric was an insult to women, it is really an accurate reflection of the dominant, male attitude had by many men all through the history of mankind.

It has been somewhat of a burden for Jimmy Page to replay and exceed the Led Zeppelin phenomenon. His personality is one of self-consciousness and he is constantly making artistic demands upon himself. He is concerned about expanding his boundaries and superseding what he has previously done. His guitar solos will always demand a spotlight because they are truly, mind boggling and impressive. It is imperative for musical bands to refrain from proscribing a lifestyle which was a large part of the appeal of grunge band, Nirvana, in which Kurt Cobain pointed fingers and made people aware of his suffering, but he, most certainly, did not pretend to have a cure for society's ills.

The guitar playing abilities of Jimmy Page have extended far beyond those required for heavy metal music to many different styles of music. During his recorded solo on the song 'Stairway to Heaven' he used a Fender Telecaster guitar and the recording itself is a very intricately produced masterpiece with scores of punch-ins. When Page played on Robert Plant's 1988 *Now and Zen* the music showed the two of them to be very modern in their own way. The Page–Plant enterprise of *No Quarter* was Romantic, fresh and new and Plant did quite well updating the vocals on old favourites such as 'Gallows Pole' and 'The Battle of Evermore'. James Patrick Page attended an art school not a fancy music school and I am not sure if his name appears in the new Encyclopaedia Britannica, but what he did with the pantothenic blues scale is Herculean historically.

In order for the heavy metal performers to attract the moneyed female audience in the next millennium it will become necessary for them to speak the language which we understand and, currently this occasion is an extreme rarity. Most of my girlfriends have been to law school and song titles like 'Upside Down Inside Out' are simply not going to force them or me to the concert arena even if our word processors collapse. Yet, most New Age artists are just too conservative. Unless the next group of aspiring heavy metal guitarists want to perpetually bond with themselves, I suggest that their lyrics and CD artwork address environmental concerns or something just as important. How about learning to play their musical instruments before boarding the stage?

Page mentioned in interviews how the placement of the microphones in front and in back of the drums during recording sessions was crucial to the sound of the early Led Zeppelin recordings: 'distance makes depth'. This is his explanation of how the band achieved their old blues sound.[1]

During the 1980s and 1990s Page carted around an old, Vox AC-30 amplifier to his dressing room at concerts. He most frequently uses it for warming up backstage. He owns a wide array of guitars and these are the ones he preferred in the 1980s:

- A red Gibson SG style, double-necked 6/12
- A Sunburst Les Paul Standard
- A black Danelectro
- A pre CBS rosewood necked, dark, brown Telecaster[2]

His 1990s 'guitar army' as he calls it is similar, but more extensive. In addition to his Whammy pedals and his theremin, he has begun to include a Soldano amp, a Peavey 5150 amplifier and a modified Fender Bassman amplifier. On his stage there is always a Marshall amp as well. Some of his newer and fancier gadgetry includes a Rane splitter, an Echoplex, a Digi Tech Legend 21 rack unit, and a Digi Tech Whammy pedal. Additional guitars used on the Coverdale Page CD included: a Gretsch Falcon, a Strat style Jackson, a Fender acoustic, and a Gibson J-200.[3]

Page had a Gibson 'Black Beauty' Les Paul custom, which he purchased in 1962, that was stolen ten years later while he toured with Led Zeppelin. His very early guitars used with The Yardbirds included a Vox 12-String and a 1958 Fender Telecaster. Other favourites of his are a Paul Reed Smith electric guitar with a tremolo bar, a Gibson A4 Mandolin, a Gibson 1920s Harp Guitar, a Rickenbacker 12-String and a Martin D28 Acoustic.

The residue of the musical legacy left by heavy-metal rock music of the 1970s turned into industrial grunge music in the 1990s and is modern folk music played at high volume with the noisy sounds of the outdoor landscape used as realistic accents. Performed by rock artists as archaic as singer Ozzy Osbourne and as fresh as singer Courtney Love and guitarist Patty Schemel in the band Hole, industrial grunge music as a vehicle for displaying emotion and communicating concerns, has become quite useful.

Autumn Garland

Nothing matures or grows old more rapidly than music. The brilliant audacity of one generation declines into the sober commonplace of another.

Sir Thomas Beecham

To be sure, Jimmy Page has enjoyed seasons of mellow fruitfulness with various artists, some who became close friends and others who remained business partners. Being a social individual he produced loud music which he hoped others would enjoy. The nature of his work kept him in the continuous process of learning and it is obvious that he had an instinct for music to have been so good, so young. Also obvious in his music and public appearances is a highly organised individual whose personality did not undergo much transformation throughout his lifetime even though he made recordings which are, each, different from each other. I miss the crowding out effect his music had on musicians before MTV. There once seemed to be room only for the most passionate of performers, then suddenly there was space for thousands of entertainers. Hunger and aggregate demand moved the economy toward full employment. It seemed richer to me when there was a deficit situation regarding rock stars.

Prior to 1957 easy listening music was most popular. Ballads of the Jazz Era and the songs of Frank Sinatra captured a large segment of the music listening audience.

When Elvis Presley sang 'Heartbreak Hotel' and later, in 1964, when the Beatles song 'Twist and Shout' shot through the air waves, rock music began to have an audience.

In 1974, in London, Jimmy Page, who was an acquaintance of folk guitarist Roy Harper, would, frequently, play folk music with him in public exhibitions. Robert Plant, who also participated in one of these events in 1974 maintained that the session lacked coherence which is often the case with impromptu sessions, but the spontaneity of folk music is what Page enjoys. One of the things which identified folk music as being such in the 1950s was an acoustic as opposed to an electric guitar sound. Page was determined to combine all types of guitar sounds into his music.

Loud, heavy, blues, rock is the music Page played to earn his living, but he played folk music for fun and many folk influences can be found in his recordings. He enjoys playing folk music because it is based on agriculturally centred values and orally transmitted traditions. Unlike traditional folk performers who step into and out of the role of performer during a concert, Page, the consummate guitar player, will rarely stop to chat with an audience. Somehow I do not see Page, ever, not even at the 1960s nightclub gigs with the Yardbirds, interrupting a performance to get a drink at the bar or to guzzle from a bottle of Jack Daniels.

In the 1960s there was a popular group of Scottish musicians who called themselves the Incredible String Band. They played folk music, exclusively and when they wanted to expand and rejuvenate their repertoire, they took trips to Morocco and Afghanistan. All good musicians love to enrich their music. Sir Page is not a rebellious individual, but he is fiercely individualistic. Through his constant experimentation he made his own sound. One of the most interesting and Romantic moments of his eclectic artistry came, in the early 1970s, when Robert Plant decided to incorporate the vocals of Sandy Denny into the *Led Zeppelin IV* song, 'The Battle of Evermore'. Ms Denny was Robert Plant's favourite British singer at the time she sang in the pioneering, electric, folk-rock group, Fairport Convention. She had an incredible talent of singing the listener into her heart and on the 'The Battle of Evermore' her vocals give the song its historical resonance. She was one of the first female, folk-rock stars and it shows the very, real, artistic acumen of Page and Plant that they captured her vocal for posterity on one of their earliest albums.

Within the CD *Led Zeppelin BBC Sessions*, of 18th November, 1997, is a subtle glimpse at the primitive, pre-conscious roots of Jimmy Page. These are all live cuts recorded during appearances the band made at the British Broadcasting Company in 1969 and 1971. Most of their early work is here in its raw, concert form along with three interviews with band members ranging from the years 1969 to 1990. Interview II from 1976 on BBC Sessions hears Jimmy Page speak of his best performances being done in a trance-like state, which is to say that it is the song which is important to him, not himself as the performer. His decision to cover Willie Dixon song selections 'You Shook Me', I Can't Quit You Baby' and 'You Need Love' illustrate this point as does the Moroccan flavouring on the *No Quarter* CD. During this interview he calls Led Zeppelin an 'earthy' band. Page and Plant both loved the way Boston folk singer, Joan Baez, covered 'Babe I'm Gonna Leave You' and this was why they chose to cover the song.

The acoustic sounds of Led Zeppelin lacked nothing in the way of being folk music and this diversification in their music added to its popularity. Because a song like 'Going To California' is such polished folk music it takes its listener to an ethereal place. I find it remarkable how the combined interests of Page and Plant blended together so seriously and yet so comfortably, but it is for this reason that the two succeeded to such an elaborate degree. It is an appropriate observation that these two are each subtly genius in their own way. The classical music genre became outdated because its fixed, structured nature did not allow for regional variations. Folk music is always regional, and is attractive to many different audiences. The most notable feature of the lyrics of folk songs is the emphasis on good faith and honesty. Folk music is similar to the blues in the way of being sincere. These qualities are apparent in the music of Jimmy Page and contribute to its lasting appeal. One of the Led Zeppelin songs that defies categorisation is 'When the Levee Breaks'. The song follows 'Going to California' on the fourth Led Zeppelin CD. The seven minute song transports me further away than any other I have ever heard.

The people of England organised the Folk-Song Society in 1898. The British have done their utmost to collect and decipher the original folk songs from their geographical area and they publish a monthly journal in which extensive collections of their pastoral folk songs, ballad sheets, carols, hunting, soldier and sea songs are published. Folk music traditionally celebrates social solidarity and community as does the Led Zeppelin classic 'Stairway to Heaven'. There are annual English folk festivals held in England. The festival at Whitby in Yorkshire usually lasts a week.

I remember the Page–Plant event, which I attended at the MGM Grand Garden with my two best friends, being a celebration where I saw many friends whom I had not seen for a long time and so, even though the concert was attended by thirteen thousand people it felt like an intimate, social experience to me. If I would have attended my four hour graduation ceremony at UNLV instead of the

Page–Plant concert, 12th May, 1995 would not have been nearly as pleasant and my evening would have been just another UNLV ordeal instead of the celebration a graduation should be. It was never a question for me at the beginning of the semester which event I would attend. I chose the one which represented a universal solidarity and love and am extremely grateful that I had a choice. However, the social identity of the other people who comprised the audience at this event was much more interesting than mine. My girlfriend, Juliette, who makes seventy-five thousand dollars a year as a cosmetologist, also attended and she bought many a piece of Page–Plant memorabilia sold at the event. Not all the fans were young Yuppies though, some were conservative pit bosses who work in gambling pits in casinos, some were budding guitarists who came to see the finest rock guitarist of our time, and all were fans of the music played by Jimmy Page. Most art forms have become commodities and I majored in English because I am an artist not because I was headed toward law school like my classmates. I would not have participated in the depersonalising graduation ceremony at UNLV even if there had been no concert to attend. I had heard the ceremony was one in which the person graduating is not actually handed their degree, but only pretends to take it. If the people who head production of the graduation show were to have actually handed out degrees, the event would have held some purpose and I might have shown up, but just to stand in line to show I went to four years of college, for me, would have been ludicrous and embarrassing.

To Page, music is a form of communication not just another entertainment to be consumed. As entertaining as Page and Plant were I left each of their 1995 concerts feeling enlightened because of the cultural shift which was expressed by the presence of several string players and the Egyptian musicians. From the historical perspective of looking at twenty-seven years of their music I find their expanded horizons awe-inspiring and I know the music which Page plays in the future will be just as impressive and stripped of bourgeois values as it always has been.

Most modern folk musicians do not feel the need to cover original folk songs, but prefer, instead, to perform new material which articulates a timeless subject matter. The folk music genre is best enjoyed in intimate settings by small audiences, but Jimmy Page has been as successful at making his new music accessible as he has been in combining his musical styles to create a convivial atmosphere at large, commercial concert events. He has always been aware of the fact that his songs will be artefacts at some point in history and this self-consciousness has led to the omnipotent feeling displayed by his music. In England, in 1998, folk music still retains a following. During the summer season music festivals such as the two-day Cropredy Festival in August and the Reading Festival, also in August, allow thousands to enjoy musical events in the open air. When Page and Plant toured the world in 1998, the Reading Festival of 28th August was one of their dates, the event was attended by forty thousand people and Page and Plant concluded the all day event which showed other bands as well. Their performance began at 9.45 p.m. and Page performed a solo during the Coverdale-Page song 'Don't Leave Me This Way' which left the audience mesmerised by his playing ability. On 6th August, 1998 Page performed at his lighting manager's wedding at the Drumquinna Hotel in Kerry, Ireland. Page and Plant performed a seven song set which began with 'I've Got A Woman' and ended with 'Mystery Train'. Casual affairs such as these to which he can take his girlfriend and children, delight Sir Page. Other August dates were the Little Big Festival in Vaduz, Switzerland on 21st August, the Bizzarre Festival in Cologne, Germany of 23rd August and the 26th August date in Dublin, Ireland.[1]

As stated earlier, Jimmy Page played on many recordings as a studio musician. Some of his studio work from the 1960s has been put together on *Session Man I* (1989) and *Session Man Vol. II* (1991). He regards the folksy blues guitarist Roy Harper very highly and he played on Harper's *Stormcock* and his 1974 *Flashes from the Archives of Oblivion*. On 6th May, 1984, Page performed with Roy Harper at the May Tree in Thetford, England and later the two recorded 'Whatever Happened to Jugula?'

A session is a term given to informal gatherings of musicians at which they meet to play. Music at these sessions is played extempore, leaving room for embellishment and improvisation. The Led Zeppelin BBC Sessions were recorded at the very time when the potential of electronic sound ornamentation was beginning to be exploited thus the songs they played were easy to reproduce during a live performance. Some of the later creations of Jimmy Page would be exceedingly difficult to do justice to in the concert arena.

The *Quarterly Musical Magazine and Review*, England's first journal dedicated to the profession of music, surfaced in the earliest part of the nineteenth century. Music then, as now, was only viewed by some as an essential art form and has, typically, been the easiest art form to exploit commercially. In the days when the piano-forte was all the rage unknown musicians were notoriously poor. One hundred years later, Sir Page was seemingly born with an innate knowledge of how to overcome that stereotype. He was paid as a studio musician when his touring musician friends were overworked and starving. Although he has become beneficent and humanitarian when it comes to helping fellow musicians, ex-wives and worthy, charitable causes, he has been known to be extremely insecure in regards to his own money and every possible dime from his musicianship has landed safely into a bank account or investment. Peter Grant and Jimmy Page were aggressively demanding when booking concert engagements, even near the beginning of their partnership. In 1972 and 1973 Led Zeppelin was being paid seventy-five thousand dollars for a one night stand. No other rock band was demanding that kind of cash in those days. Grant and Page did much to define the rock act as commercial commodity.

Folk music of the 1990s was as dizzyingly diverse as the many people who played it and had made a minute, coffee house type of resurgence in certain parts of America during this decade. Purity of heart and of purpose must be audible so as to define it as folk music. Odetta, Judy Collins, Pete Seeger, Bob Dylan, and James Taylor all made major contributions to this genre of music.

The Economy of Listening

*If the doors of perception were cleansed every thing would
appear to man as it is, infinite.*

William Blake

So many days have gone by, since Jimmy Page and Robert
Plant began musically singeing their way into my
consciousness. There are three books bearing the titles
Stairway to Heaven. The one authored by Richard Cole
and Richard Trubo is called *Stairway to Heaven: Led Zeppelin
Uncensored* and was quite enjoyable for me to read because I
discovered even more things which Page and I have in
common. As adolescents we both enjoyed peregrination.
He hitchhiked across India after touring with the
Yardbirds. At sixteen, I joined the International Society for
Krishna Consciousness temple in Culver City, California.
Since then I have been everywhere and so has Jimmy Page.
There have been two other brave souls to title their books
Stairway to Heaven and both are brilliant works. The one
called *The Stairway to Heaven* was written by Sitchin
Zecharia and contains earth chronicles. The one by Davin
Seay is called *Stairway to Heaven: The Spiritual Roots of Rock
n' Roll from the King and Little Richard to Prince and Amy
Grant*. This book gives a three-page analysis of Led
Zeppelin and tells of the home of Page, called Tower
House, having a Catholic confessional.

In 1900, in Mexico, Aleister Crowley began to explore the value of yoga as an exercise in controlling the mind. Later, in 1937, he gave eight lectures on yoga in London. This type of belief system is responsible for preserving the health of Jimmy Page in the 1990s. Page eats really well, a truly, balanced vegetarian diet, gets exercise and has an optimistic mental outlook. He takes acupuncture on occasion and avoids any stressful interaction with human beings who do not please him. Although he has struggled with his belief system he is a Christian. Jimmy Page loves life which is not to say he is not moody or he never gets depressed. He is moody and very serious, but he had much to look forward to in 1998 and so did his fans. On the stage at Shoreline in Mountain View, California, I witnessed Page as an affectionate and gentle guitar player. However, my earlier impression of him at the May show was of an arrogant, self-centred, sombre, unprincipled individual who lacked respect for his audience because he smoked on stage. The additional autumn glimpses I had of him while seated with his acoustic guitar showed a gentler and, certainly, a more obliging side of his personality. I was in such close proximity to him on the night of 7th October, 1995, I felt his stage fright as he was about to perform and it astonished me. This elderly gentleman, with his childlike ways, who has been declared by many to be the greatest guitar player who has ever lived, stood petrified in the dark before he began his performance and inhaled cigarette smoke deeply. His artistic and sensitive nature was very apparent in 1995 and all the public acclaim he has had during his lifetime has begun to reassure him.

Lisa Robinson, who wrote about Led Zeppelin all through their career, was just as dazzled by their music as the rest of us. She wrote articles for *Disc*, *Rolling Stone* and a column for the *New York Post*. In 1973 she described their act as leaving you breathless and always wanting more.

Page music is chameleon-like, like the universe and yet the audience can always expect an immensely, powerful sound to emanate from a Page–Plant show. The form of ethnic revival on the 1998 *Walking Into Clarksdale* is blues music. This new music is rustic, like burnished mahogany and authentic because of their thirty years of experience.

What Page and Plant had going for them, publicity wise, on their 1995 tour was two-fold. They drew a crowd of diverse ages to the arena, some of which were people who were familiar with their music, but were just a trifle too young to have caught Led Zeppelin in concert. Our curiosity was titanic. The New Age strangeness of their Moroccan flavoured *No Quarter* CD drew their long-time fans, people who had nothing better to do that night, and people who love world music that has a universal appeal. This time, however, people will attend a Page–Plant show because they know the two gentlemen to be the most discriminating of the dinosaur rock acts.

In March of 1998 Jimmy Page sojourned in Brazil. He loved a twenty-two-year-old Argentinean girl named Jemena and her two-year-old daughter. His nature is spiritual, so he loved giving up his London real estate when he headed for any rural retreat he could find. It seems Page has remained the loving, impressionable, naive, trusting soul and at the age of fifty-four a landscape filled with sunshine brightens his every day. Choosing to leave the rainy environment in England and the British monarchy, with its governing parliament and reputation for taxing citizens to an exorbitant degree, was a healthy way to relieve his worrying spirit. To avoid enormous tax expenditures it is required of those British citizens who have high incomes to spend a minimum of six months each year in another country. Ever the economiser, Page bought a piece of Lencois land for thirty-five thousand reais.[1]

Sir Page owns a condominium in Nevada and when he is not residing in his native country he enjoys some of his brooding moments looking across the misty lake and landscape of the tenth wealthiest community of the United States where his melancholy spirit is soothed by the fact that he has accomplished much, musically, during his lifetime. In England his homes lulled him into meditative states with their deep, green valleys. The hazy fields and the many hills of England inspired his music. The heroic battles which occurred there in the centuries preceding his birth gave him much to contemplate when he was in quest of upward mobility. Internationally famous for the last twenty-five years of the twentieth century he was unusually astute at avoiding unnecessary publicity and in maintaining his privacy. When not on tour or involved in recording efforts he enjoys night-clubbing and listening to musicians play. By choosing to live in places where over-population cannot bother him, such as Brazil, he can play out the role of the old and wise village shaman. He loves meeting new people and he endears himself to people immediately because of his easy-going, gentle manners.

Wherever the next hundred years takes us in music and literature, Jimmy Page influenced the musical road to the future and manoeuvred in the Romantic genre of music in a stunning manner. Percy Bysshe Shelley was also a serious and passionate artist who dreamed about making the world a better place. Though both Page and Shelley were once considered radicals, their important contributions to the arts are noticeable. Loving a refined ideal is what motivated Shelley to write poetry, Page to play music and me to write this book. Like the work of Shelley, the songs of Page were defined by their tenacious intensity. Both had their religious beliefs held under scrutiny and criticised at least once during their lives. Unlike Shelley, Jimmy Page was extremely popular during his lifetime. The tone colour of two or three musical notes played by Jimmy Page sets a mood instantly, it is frightening to feel the feelings he can provoke with just two of his notes.

Guitar playing became a very popular hobby during the twentieth century. In the July 1997 magazine *How to Play Guitar* was an instructional text with an accompanying CD. In this issue the music of Jimmy Page is used for instruction. Here on track four, 'Jimmy's Back pages', it is obvious that these lessons are for knowledgeable and well-practised guitar players and the music of Page is unrecognisable in most of these chord snippets. It is intricate and complicated music even for people who read music.

Crowds of tens of thousands of people are easily influenced by propaganda, music and human passions. This has been demonstrated time and again throughout history. Obviously, this mob mentality was demonstrated in Hitler's Germany of the 1920s and 1930s, but just as obvious of what Aldous Huxley called 'herd poisoning' have been the hordes of concert-goers who love to worship at the altar we call a stage, seemingly, anyone who entertains on a stage. This romantic phenomenon is not a unique product of the twentieth century, but years of doubling human population have made the new numbers in audience crowds most significant. What is also significant are the entertaining techniques and personality traits used by popular singers and lyricists during the twentieth century. Although the team of Page and Plant did not obtain an outstanding or superior education they consider themselves highly intelligent and, in general, have thought themselves superior to the masses they influenced. With fame came money and in 1998 Page and Plant are still impressed with how much money they are able to extract, from thousands of people, with a tour and a couple of new songs. Plant has screamed and wailed on the stage as has a guitar played by Jimmy Page. These types of performances excite emotions in the nightly crowds and people love to feel strong emotions. These performers were not required to write oratories which made logical sense, their lyrics or speeches only had to captivate. Plant and Page had an easy time in this captivation since they did not have to perpetrate brainwashing techniques or force to inspire loyalty and trust in their fans. The audience of Led Zeppelin was perfectly willing to wash their own brains with an array of available drugs like which the world had never seen until the 1970s. To say their success was coterminous with the decay of their societies would be to simplify human behaviour and as neatly as the statement would fit in this context it would not be entirely accurate. Page simply enjoyed his ability to entertain large masses of people. The arenas in which he performed in 1998 all had minimum seating capacities of ten thousand people.

From producing blues albums at Andrew Loog Oldham's Immediate Records in 1964 to entertaining thousands of people through the 1970s, 1980s, and 1990s, Jimmy Page allowed himself to become morose over the loss of his friend, John Bonham, but he also allowed himself to become re-inspired to make great music again in the 1990s with Robert Plant. Cementing their amazing, musical relationship is the 1998 CD *Walking Into Clarksdale*. Life is really good for fans of Jimmy Page in 1998. Page and Plant launched a fifty city tour which began on 21st February in Zagreb, Croatia where ten thousand tickets were sold. Monday, 23rd February had them in a Sports Hall in Budapest, Hungary, Wednesday, 25th February in Prague. An appearance in Bucharest, Romania followed a date in Poland then they performed in Sofia, Bulgaria. 5th and 6th March saw them in Istanbul, Turkey. On the first day of spring I heard news of their summer tour on Dave

Linwood's Tight But Loose site on the Internet relating to Page and Plant and it was a great time to be alive.

Walking Into Clarksdale, released on 21st April, 1998, features Arabic influence on the hard rocking single 'Most High', but that only begins to describe the song. In an interview Plant gave in Sofia he said the song 'Sons of Freedom' is about religious and cultural repression. Plant has become concerned about injustices in the world which do not affect him personally. The rest of the lyrics show Plant in search of answers to his questions about why the righteous suffer. It is amazing to me how talented the two are together, this song feels so good. The month of May of 1998 began with the pair of Page and Plant touring, beginning with four dates in Florida. Drummer Michael Lee and bassist Charlie Jones began backing Robert Plant in 1993 and went on Plant's Fate of Nations tour, the two also assisted on the No Quarter tour in 1995. In 1998 Plant and Page tossed in keyboard player Phil Andrews to join them on the road. In early 1998 live performances they gave in Europe relied almost totally on songs from the Led Zeppelin catalogue with the exceptions of the new 'Most High', 'Walking Into Clarksdale' and 'Shining In the Light'. The music of the 1995 tour expanded their reach and the 1998 tour, sees them doing what they enjoy most: expanding blues, rock genres. In June they explored the South further by playing in Alabama, Tennessee, Oklahoma, and Missouri. On 4th July they performed in Toronto, Canada. Their 1998 concert set list featured that fat sound of theirs again.

There are twelve new songs on the *Walking Into Clarksdale* CD and on the song 'Sons of Freedom' Jimmy Page plays a six-stringed bass guitar. The song collection was recorded at London's famous Abbey Road studios and mastered at the Pink Room in Twickenham at the home studio of Jon Astley. Most men over the age of thirty whom I have met get tired sooner or later, but Jimmy Page and Robert Plant show no sign of getting lazy or uncreative on *Walking Into Clarksdale*. It had been four years since *No Quarter* which consisted, mostly, of Led Zeppelin songs remade. The three new songs: 'Yallah', 'Wonderful One' and 'City Don't Cry', are songs which unfortunately were not immediately grasped by the American audience, which though Page and Plant would be loathe to admit it, have been the major purchasers of their music. 'Yallah' means let's go somewhere around Marrakech, and the Moroccan people must have been delighted to see Page and Plant performing in their own desert sands in 1995. This new product put out by the duo, the first complete collection of new songs from this pair in eighteen years. My favourite song here is 'When I was a child' in which the lyric talks to everyone and the guitar music will never be surpassed. As inspirational titles go 'Walking Into Clarksdale' is cute because Plant tells us he was born to be a blues singer and makes us believe it. Clarksdale refers to a town in Mississippi where blues music was quite popular in the 1930s. Taking the blues in their own direction on this CD, are the adventures of Page with Plant, where pretence gives in to talent. 'Please Read The Letter' has an ardent feeling and the guitar intro sounds like my fifteen-year-old next-door neighbour, who aspires to be the next great guitarist. 'Blue Train' is the song Jim Morrison would be singing if he were alive today and Plant is calm as he breathes love lost, in combination with the song 'When the World was Young', Plant has become so effective as a soul singer that he is suddenly, capable of making me cry. Within the song 'Walking Into Clarksdale' and most of the other songs here is a depth of wilderness and emotion and I realise, once again, why I am obsessed with calling their music Romantic. My terminology should be confused and intermingled with any feelings which are passionate, confusing, overwhelming and inspired because that is their music. The serious natures of Page and Plant do not allow their listeners to be cheerful anymore. The two musicians were sober during the creation of this music, but for me it is somewhat serious, but, simultaneously, uplifting.

On 15th April,1998 the premiere broadcast of 'Walking Into Clarksdale' went out to Americans on two hundred and twenty radio stations. Disc jockey Jill Robinson interviewed Page and Plant and the show concluded with Robert Plant flirting with the hostess. It was nice to know these old guys still had some life in them because Plant's sexuality is no longer the basis of his appeal in the music and he has become somewhat of an intellectual. The listener can even make sense of most of his lyrics here. Page was his usual affected and opinionated self during this interview. He has always impressed audiences with his mastery of the blues and his versatility in mixing different musical styles. I hope this book laid emphasis on the inspiration which musicians who love their craft provide.

The Making of a Hit Record

Art is not a handicraft, it is the transmission of feeling the artist has accumulated.

Leo Tolstoy

The most famous pieces of Romantic music were written by Berlioz, Chopin, Mendelssohn, Schumann, Liszt, Brahms, Rachmaninov, Mahler and Richard Strauss. Page emulated Presley and other musicians of his era and the music of each sounded completely different just as happened with Beethoven and Bruckner. Page used his music as an expression of the inexpressible. He became a rock and roll overlord as he used any and all resources which were available to him. He gained momentum in his musical output because he kept his vision big. Like the earlier, Romantic composers he did not waste his talent in a reproduction of the average, daily life of human beings, but instead his music displayed a kaleidoscopic view of what people are capable of feeling and how broad their range of expression can be. In the world of Page love is a pure, creative happiness that he shows by playing music.[1]

Ludwig Van Beethoven was born in 1770 during the peak years of the classical period of music, but in the midst of many a piano virtuoso of whom Haydn and Mozart were two and during the eighteenth century classical music was the only popular genre of music. Page, however, began his musical career when there were few guitar masters.

154

Consequently, Page was vital to twentieth-century guitar music. During the 1990s his audience felt grateful that his output was forthcoming and exquisite; we were happy with the Led Zeppelin catalogue of music and none of us expected him to surpass it. After his first two blues-based recordings he was never in danger of being derivative and he took inspiration for his music from his natural surroundings and from watching his children. It was when he passed the age of fifty that he began to feel comfortable in the role of professional musician, but he never had an unanxious moment about his music. Page lived with a feeling of obligation to create from the very moment he began playing guitar.

Musical soundtracks began to dominate CD sales during the 1990s and many of the finest musicians sold their works in this format. Here is a list of genres of music which were most popular during June of 1998: Motion Picture Soundtracks, Country, Rap, Hip-Hop, Alternative, Blues, Rock, New Age, Pop and Latin. Page stuck like glue to rock and blues and enriched the tone-colour palette of each. *Walking Into Clarksdale* is Page and Plant in first gear of their new career. This music is full of the finesse and confidence of Jimmy Page, is not overly stimulating and most of the melodies are emotive.[2]

I attended my fourth Page–Plant show in Oklahoma City, Oklahoma on 4th June, 1998. They began their performance with classics from the 1970s: 'Bring It On Home', 'Heartbreaker' and 'Ramble On'. The new songs they performed this night were 'Walking Into Clarksdale', 'Heart In your Hand', 'Most High' and 'Shining In The Light' with no nods to their solo careers. Plant sang an irritatingly, slow version of Led Zeppelin's originally upbeat 'Down By The Seaside'. It seemed as if he was trying to unstimulate this audience who were extremely sedate to begin with. Everywhere I stood there was a smoker and by the time the show ended, exactly two hours after it began at 9 p.m., the Myriad arena was full of pot and tobacco smoke. Jimmy Page felt the need to don a white cowboy hat for the encore songs, 'Thank You' and 'Rock and Roll', he smoked cigarettes every time he switched guitars, he seemed grumpy as he stomped around the stage in his black outfit and there were no flirtatious smiles towards me during his performance; Robert Plant commented to the audience, that he had fallen in love and that was the extent of their charm toward the audience. The two were completely dressed in black clothing, Page immaculately and Plant as if he had just jumped out of the sea, and they merely performed their job, nothing more.

Robert Plant made a large contribution to the phenomenon of success which enveloped Jimmy Page during the twentieth century and when talking about the personalities and the music of Jimmy Page and Robert Plant it is easy to see that the workmanship comes from Page and much of the bohemian creativity from Plant who performed in blues bands Black Snake Moon, The Banned, Listen and Band of Joy before meeting Jimmy Page in 1968. To take a look at the solo careers of each is to see that Page felt it necessary to have famous people involved in his four, solo endeavours: *The Firm*, *Mean Business*, *Outrider* and *Coverdale Page* and that Robert Plant started from scratch. The lyric writer of the two, when working together, was Robert Plant, beginning with his conception of the song 'Stairway to Heaven'. Highly energetic and always thinking, Robert Plant, began his solo career with Pictures at Eleven in 1982 which debuted at number two in the United Kingdom and *The Principle of Moments* in 1983. He began his solo touring career in August of 1983 and then released the following musical albums with unknown musicians: *The Honey Drippers*, *Shaken and Stirred*, *Now and Zen*, *Manic Nirvana* and *Fate Of Nations*.[3, 4]

An enjoyable look at some of the song lyrics which Plant wrote during his lifetime would include song one from the 1988 *Now and Zen*, 'Heaven Knows'. In the song he asks what kind of fool he is and so I will answer his question. Plant who was born in August of 1948, is like the sun that is big, radiant, strong and warm. He is sometimes self-indulgent and he is always over-confident. Song two here is titled 'Dance On My Own' and is Plant obsessing over a girl, something he has done persistently throughout his lifetime, although with an infinite variety of women. 'Tall Cool One' is the great rocker from this collection and the lyrics make reference to him being like a cat. It is a natural reference since he was born during the sign of Leo on 20th August, the last day of the lionine zodiacal influence. It seems he wants to love everyone. He uses snippets of guitar licks played by Page for the songs 'Whole Lotta Love', 'Dazed and Confused', 'Custard Pie' and 'The Ocean'. I find this insertion of Page music into his own to be a necessary tribute to the talent that is Jimmy Page. There was no chance in 1982 that Page and Plant would reunite and play old Led Zeppelin songs on a tour. Plant was uninterested in it and Page was still morose over the loss of John Bonham.

Several of the lyrics of Robert Plant such as those in 'The Way I Feel' prove to me that he has made efforts to defy the alcoholic, wanton and promiscuous stereotype of rock stars who were famous during the 1980s. Also in 'The Way I Feel' is his expression of concern over the way his face looks. I must state here that the image of Plant at the 1998 Oklahoma City concert showed me one of the most interesting faces full of rich character I had ever seen in my lifetime. His is the face of a person who has fought serious wars within himself and, perhaps, won some of them through will power and endurance. With such a cheerful and outgoing personality as he has, I do not think it matters how many wrinkles he has. 'Helen of Troy' is about a women of modern times whom Plant would clearly like to admire. The lyrics of Plant always concern themselves with a strange and detached kind of love.

Plant's song 'Ship of Fools' begins with him talking about his heart breaking. The title Ship of Fools has a long tradition beginning with the German book *Das Narrenschiff* which was written by Sebastian Brent between the years 1458 and 1521. A newer book bearing the title of *Ship of Fools* was written by Katherine Anne Porter and published in 1945.[5] The song 'White Clean and Neat' is similar to 'Walking Into Clarksdale' in that in both songs Plant thinks back to when he was five years old and both are about music and musicians. During his recording career with Led Zeppelin, Robert Plant wrote songs in which he seemed to be begging for sex and he has always, instinctively known the principles of persuasive communication. His lyrics, nearly always, refer to the female 'you' in either an overtly sexual or emotional prayer. The study of persuasive tactics in communication goes as far back as 928 BC when Plato was born.

The *Walking Into Clarksdale* CD contains some of the finest lyrics Plant has ever written, on the CD and in performance, he is in character talking about light, reincarnation and love. To understand Robert Plant it is important to have, at least, a minimal knowledge of the beliefs of Celtic Britain because the beliefs of those times are what allowed his imagination to draw upon when writing songs throughout his career with Jimmy Page. The song 'Upon a Golden Horse', while barely comprehensible, exhibits the thoughts he enjoys. The Celts had their own Saints and Saint Patrick, the one whom James Patrick Page gets his middle name from was one of the most internationally famous because he brought the Christian religion to Ireland. The culture of the Celts was entirely inundated with nature and trees. They believed that the unseen world affected the invisible world of matter and they held women in as high esteem as men as shown by their worship of gods and goddesses. Saint Brigid was worshipped at the fire festival during February.[6]

'Blue Train', 'Heart in Your Hand' and 'Please Read The Letter' are as close as the band gets to playing love songs on *Walking Into Clarksdale*. In 'Please Read The Letter' Plant is as casual about the break-up of a relationship as he would be the breaking of a tennis racket and the line: 'There's nothing here that's left for you, but check with lost and found', tries so hard to be cool, that it is kind of nauseating. I am left to wonder why should he or she read the letter? No matter, the rest of the CD is comprised of interesting and powerful music and these songs are as captivating as any of the Led Zeppelin songs. Although the lyrics are redundant in that irritating Plant delivery, the music is droning in that curative Moroccan mode, the song, 'Most High', made sense as a hit single during the summer of 1998, as a logical follow-up to their 1994 mid-Eastern *No Quarter* project. The title track 'Walking Into Clarksdale' is great and has everything it needs including Page playing a casual and cool blues with his guitar slung low. My favourite song is 'When I was a Child' because it confirms what I knew to be true about the childhood of Jimmy Page when I began writing this book, that he slept at heaven's gate.

When I played guitar, from 1978 until 1988, my musical practice consisted of a daily battle of trying to make new sounds with the same tired, old six strings, a stand-off which the guitar usually won by ending up in the corner silent. Consequently, I find it remarkable how Page, who began playing twenty years earlier than I did, when there was little rock guitar music on record, pulled an immensely, diverse array of sounds from his guitar and made it look and feel so effortless.

Appealing to a wide segment of the musical audience is present, but not uppermost in the minds of Page and Plant when producing a musical product which is why there is a delicate balance on *Walking Into Clarksdale*. The song collection consists of blues, grunge-metal, mid-Eastern cymbal and drum sounds in a subtle statement of musical evolution and with this eclecticism they interest rockers of all ages, blues buffs and people over fifty years of age who respect Page and Plant simply for their staying power. Banning sexual stereotypes, implementing spiritual sound bites, creating unique musical motifs, combining physical strength and endurance with professional musicianship are the talents of Page and Plant that keep people going to a Page–Plant show and buying their music.

I wrote this book and then, on the night of the autumnal equinox in 1998, Page and Plant in all their glory returned to Las Vegas, Nevada. Very vaguely, the concert stirred up inherent admiration for Jimmy Page and his natural playing ability. I loved the sloppy way in which he delivered the old, Led Zeppelin song 'Babe I'm Gonna Leave You' and the flawless 'Going To California'. I would have appreciated a song or two from the solo careers of Robert Plant and Jimmy Page maybe even a cover song or two, but this tour stressed, clearly, components of the twenty-eight-year-old Led Zeppelin repertoire. The alternatives came when the band performed 'When the World was Young', 'Heart In Your Hand', 'Walking Into Clarksdale' and 'Most High'. The lusty environment and the diversity of their music was being engraved into the audience's memory by the time they concluded their show with 'Whole Lotta Love' which was as intense as it had to be to enliven the humans in the crowd. Because Page, at fifty-four years of age, was such a beautiful specimen of masculinity, he was quite effective as a rock guitarist. His black, cashmere sweater, sleek, black slacks and black Doc Marten shoes comprised the understated and elegant attire which he wore during every performance of this tour. When the set was over and the audience screamed for more, it was thrilling to use the last two songs, 'Thank You' and 'Rock and Roll' to glimpse the illustrious Page before he flew off to show other cacti, snakes and humans his musical exhibitions.

My battery went dead in my camera as I was about to snap a second photo of my darling hero, but I took one so my reader is able to obtain a very clear glimpse of Page with his Gibson Sunburst, taken Wednesday, 23rd September, 1998 at the MGM Grand Garden. Page utilised his motivation to perform in sixteen countries in 1998 and from Las Vegas he went directly to Phoenix, Arizona. There is no substitute for his kind of music for me, his is far superior to the music of the other fossil bands such as Blue Oyster Cult or Deep Purple. Part of the society in 1998 regarded his music as important for there was an ongoing purchase of two million Led Zeppelin records annually and an increased awareness of the *Walking Into Clarksdale* CD occurred as the Page–Plant band concluded their 1998 North American tour on 2nd October in Memphis, Tennessee.

To address the personality of Page as I viewed it this night: it pictured a mature man with the innocence of a child, a more pampered human being would be difficult to find. This is part of why he has been capable of giving his musically, important resource so consistently. He has never attracted fans because of a distressing message as many try to do today. His music and the lyrics of Robert Plant tend to concentrate on the love of angelic beings and marriages in heaven between angels and kings. The layout promoting this tour and CD consisted of the faces of two young boys lacing their bold wings together. The human eye is drawn to their innocence and perfection and insatiable audience curiosity is satisfied. In fact audience satisfaction is what Jimmy Page spent the year of 1998 giving.

Remains of the Day

Once you have the bottom there, you can go anywhere.
The more doubts and negatives you knock out of anything,
the heavier it gets.

Jimi Hendrix

On the evening of 7th October, 1998 I attended a preview performance of a show called O at the Bellagio Hotel in my hometown of Las Vegas, Nevada. The show could not have been more exquisitely Romantic in its display of water escapades, ballet dancing and music. On the stage this night more than two dozen dancers threw flames and danced skilfully and wildly. The music combined East Indian, Moroccan, African, Oriental and Italian motifs and a female guitarist played flamenco music on an acoustic guitar in a glassed room to the right of the stage. Rain over dancers dressed like Zebras, swimming and fun and precise acrobatics comprised the show given by the Cirque du Soleil dance troupe. The water stage held a piano, a floating rock holding clowns, and the ballet acrobats captivated each viewer of the fifteen hundred in the audience for ninety minutes. The show does not pretend to represent modern reality, the show wants its audience to escape for a while.

Popular today is a musical genre that is not based on fantasy, in fact, it revels in the realistic and that is hip-hop. It is possible that I have not covered the truth of the Romantic phenomenon that enveloped James Patrick Page.

The thing is the time was and that time is no longer. Now is different than before and Jimmy Page has tried recently, however feebly, to connect himself to the present by forging a musical relationship with rapper, hip-hop artist extraordinaire, Puff Daddy, who like many other hip-hop artists has conquered the world by gaining respect. Hip-hop music wants to ensure that the imagination of primitive human beings survives. By primitive I mean, non-factory worker mankind. Irony is pleasantly visible when one realises how smart the majority of these African-American, hip-hop artists are, since this ethnic group has been trampled on in America for an unbelievably long time and in spite of their lack of luck produce a musical genre so honest, innocent and innovative that it ignites interest universally. Lest I digress, hip-hop artists have been successful in turning the heads of the staid economic specialists in the music business. The modern hip-hop artists have their own recording companies and they have no need to run for shelter to a Motown or Stax record company executive in order to create, consequently, this means they have their own set of rules.

Hip-hop music is about communication before entertainment. Communication among people and I am one of these people. Hip-hop is about murdered relatives and loved ones and no one dares to obstruct or obfuscate its message. Hip-hop is about believing in God, oneself and one's fellow man. It dictates everything and cuts down boundaries. It is complicated, concise, Romantic and at this writing unrefined. It revels in the glory of if God is for you, no one can be against you. If you think you are tough you have never heard Missy Elliot lay it down.

In the middle of the 1960s, Jimmy Page went out into the world with a strong belief in himself. He held no other strong belief system, but was heavily armed with self-confidence and there were few obstacles in the way of his success. He placed himself first in all of his interactions with people. Varied older people have purchased *Walking Into Clarksdale*, but his latest seems boring to young audiences, since walking is an acquired taste, most youngsters like to run. Mystery themes are no longer more important than others and this comes through in his new music and lyrics. The world has six billion people in it in 1998 and young generations want to live well, but first and foremost we want this for everyone not just for some. Unlike country music or the other popular musical genres, generally, hip-hop music cuts through pretence and so-called talent and gets to the heart of existence which is: only the strong survive. This music wants its audience to dance, to celebrate life and to get rid of the trash. So the *Walking Into Clarksdale* CD hung in Billboard's Top Forty Albums chart for three weeks, but the *Godzilla* soundtrack (which contains the Puff Daddy/Page duet 'Come with Me') hung in for seven weeks.

I had the pleasure of attending four great concerts during the summer of 1998. The first of these was Eric Clapton's stellar sell-out show at the MGM Grand arena on 30th May, 1998. He opened his set with 'My Father's Eyes' and with this song proved that feelings about fathers are universal. His concert was not a robotic repeat of old hit songs, instead his songs expressed the deluge of love and knowledge he has accumulated during his fifty years on earth. He played 'Change the World', 'Tears in Heaven', and 'Layla' on an acoustic guitar and then satisfied and dazzled each audience member with his perfect guitar playing and passionate singing. It should not be discounted that he does both very well and these allow him to fully express himself in a balanced way. On this night he held back nothing from the people who love him as this century's premiere blues guitarist.

Saturday, 11th July, 1998 held another kind of musical fun as I showed up at 11 p.m. to watch alternative-rock band Pearl Jam hit the stage. Their concert, at the Thomas & Mack arena, had three warm up acts one of which was X, the popular, punk band from the 1980s. I am a bit claustrophobic so did not show up at the arena until singer Eddie Vedder, guitarist Mike Mcready, lead-guitarist Stone Gossard, drummer Jack Irons and bassist Jeff Agent were scheduled to perform. They played 'M.C.', 'Corduroy', 'Brain of J', 'Hail, Hail' and then the song I came to hear, 'Given to Fly'. The song bears no resemblance to Led Zeppelin's 'Going to California', but the litigious Page and Plant claim that Vedder and Gossard have leached it off of their own tribute to Joni Mitchell. After 'Given to Fly', the band really rocked for the rest of the night with songs I was familiar with like 'Dissident', 'Faithful', 'Wish list', 'Better Man, 'Jeremy'. This band has done a lot for 1990s rock and they have tried to do what they could for charitable causes such as People for the Ethical Treatment of Animals. A really good time was had by the twenty thousand or more people who bought tickets to see Pearl Jam.

I will always save the best for last when I talk about the musical artists I love most. On Saturday, 25th July, 1998 Ms Stevie Nicks appeared at the MGM Grand Garden arena in full regalia of her beauty and talent. This was the sixth time I had seen and heard her sing and it was delightful. This tour she called the Enchanted tour. As she sang and conversed with the audience I realised how fortunate I was to be listening to the most talented female rock star of our time. She blazed through three ballads 'Outside the Rain', 'Dreams' and 'Enchanted' and she sang a triad of songs from the days she was a partner to Fleetwood Mac guitarist, Lindsay Buckingham: 'After the Glitter Fades', 'Garbo' and 'Rose Garden'. She relayered her beautiful, beaded, chiffon outfits periodically throughout her set and when she returned to the stage she rocked everybody with the songs 'Stand Back' and 'Rhiannon'. After introducing her back-up singers and the musicians in her band, one of whom was keyboard-player, Brett Tuggle, who played with David Coverdale and Jimmy Page on their brief tour of Japan in 1993, the darling Stevie Nicks concluded her show with 'Whole Lotta Trouble', 'Landslide' and 'Edge of 17'. After a thundering applause she returned to perform an encore of 'I Need To Know' and her emotional tribute to the thousands who love her, 'Has Anyone Ever Written Anything For You?'.

Exactly two months later, on 26th September, 1998, three days after the Page–Plant show, I was able to see Ms Nicks again. This performance at the MGM grand arena was part of an annual benefit for charity concert arranged by the André Agassi Foundation. This event is called the 'Grand Slam For Children'. Stevie Nicks began this event with the Romantic ballad 'At Last', a song which few, if any, members of the audience knew. Of course this did not matter at all because it was Stevie Nicks, singing all dressed in aubergine like an angel dazzling all within her realm. Later she returned to give the spotlight its proper focus, midway through the show, and was joined by best friend and drummer Mick Fleetwood to play her hit songs 'Dreams', Rhiannon' and 'Stand Back'. Ms Nicks respectfully referred to my hometown of Las Vegas, Nevada as 'The City of Dreams'. I liked that because it proves she believes it is possible to live in a dream world no matter where you are.

The amazing counterpart to the Page phenomenon Jimi Hendrix, was quite the opposite of Page in many ways. Hendrix was willing to give all he had in order to communicate and, therefore, burnt himself into the American psyche before he succumbed to an accidental overdose in 1970. He made several covers of *Rolling Stone* magazine, four of which were during his short lifetime: January 1968, March 1968, February 1969 and May of 1969. Both Jimmy Page and Jimi Hendrix made their professional concert debuts in 1966. So there they were, the two most prolific guitarists of the twentieth century, standing neck in neck in London in 1967. Without benefit of education or cultural opportunity, Hendrix impressed the world immediately upon adulthood, one of two who gave everything so as to leave an impression on the musical art world at it loudest and most prolific time. Page did all that was necessary to ensure his own excellence and survival in the viper den that was the music business. Hendrix was ridden through his stardom as a clothes horse and malnourished and drug-addled victim of the drug era. Before Hendrix was the Experience he had a band he sometimes called the Rainflowers and later Jimmy James and the Blue Flames. However he managed to leave his powerful, musical manifesto behind he did so. The man who could play three guitar parts at once enjoyed some fame for three years. The singing voice of Hendrix was ultra-sincere, in 'Hey Joe' we felt him pleading his case of love lost, in 'Wild Thing' he moved us, and in his coverage of Dylan's 'Like A Rolling Stone' he moved us further from the material realm, into the one of universal feeling, than anyone previously had. Possessing a more decisively and controlled, split personality than Hendrix, Page achieved more because he never felt like he reached the mountain top. Hendrix wanted to achieve more after his arrival at the 1967 Monterey Pop Festival and his four recordings, but he did not survive to listen. Both were childlike, but Page is and has been since birth, an adult. Both fell in harm's way, but only Page survived. Genius seems most spectacular when it is fraught with insecurities as was that Hendrix, possessed, however, the light of genius is not dimmed by surefootedness and confidence.

The Octavia, a sound effect device created for Jimi Hendrix by British Naval scientist, Roger Mayer, creates a second set of notes one octave apart from the ones played. It was special effects like the Octavia which tied the music of Jimmy Page and that of Jimi Hendrix together in the late 1960s. This usage of special effects, fuzz boxes, tremolo arms and other technological gadgetry would leave far reaching effects on rock music well through the end of the century. Even Eric Clapton picked them up and played with them for a moment, but the music of Clapton eventually came clean, that of Page never did. Like a playful child he loved his noisy toys.

Jimmy Page, always a master of disguise, has maintained an existence at a superficial, earthly level, which is why he loved to create discontinuous blues riffs and enjoyed watching others display their feelings for him while he paraded intact. Hendrix, however, exposed himself and hung himself out to dry every time he hopped on stage. Past fifty, Page is gorgeous, chubby, cheerful, healthy and in love. Hendrix at twenty-six was anaemic, tired, old, depressed and, apparently, without anyone to look after him. With only a moderate show of excess during the 1970s, and in the 1990s always with restraint, Page won and *Walking Into Clarksdale* and the accompanying Walking Into Everywhere tour of 1998 affirmed this. Myopic in its discovery, like this book, *Walking Into Clarksdale*, tells little, yet tells the whole story.

Larry Rodgers interviewed Page for *The Arizona Republic* on 5th September, 1998 and during the interview Page told him that touring is something he needs to do, it is part of his addictive personality and that he enjoys the feelings of performing live. So we are left to attribute the extraordinary success of his career to an addictive personality. Actually, I think that statement is accurate. If he had not been so obsessed with his music would we be so attracted to it? It definitely pays to be obsessed with one's passions especially when those passions delight so many people. Passionate love is always the best kind. The song I remember most at the Autumn 1998 Page–Plant show is 'Babe I'm Gonna Leave You'. Folk singer, Joan Baez, covered the song which was written by folkster, Anne Bredon, during the 1960s. Page and Plant did a passionate job of covering the song in performance: it was as if Robert Plant sincerely felt homesick when he cried he had to go and Sir Page was overworking his guitar as usual.[1]

In May of 1995 Page engaged me in a process of inquiry, analysis, discipline and decision-making that gave me a Master's degree in Sir James Patrick Page. No small accomplishment was this engagement considering my excessive boredom with and detachment from everyone and everything. He left me in trust of this written work. I am merely a dancing tree fairy who came in from the woods long enough to fulfil my obligation to challenge the next millennium to rival the Romantic phenomenon of Jimmy Page.

In the song 'Most High', singer Robert Plant wants God to show a presence. My answer to Plant's question of 'Who hides the east from the blind man's eye?' is: we humans usually hide the truth from ourselves and each other. An honest person is difficult to find these days, but not impossible. I should also advise Plant that it is probable that he will find answers to his most pressing questions in places such as backstage at a Tori Amos concert, where Plant and Amos were photographed together in Los Angeles in October of 1998. At least he is looking in the right places, and he is such a friendly guy, he is bound to find his answers sooner or later. The logical would conclude that Plant is making reference to King David of the Bible in 'Most High', but considering the occupation of Robert Plant he is most probably referring to billionaire recording executive and mogul David Geffen who has been producing and buying and selling musicians since the 1960s. It was under the Geffen label that the *Outrider* and *Coverdale Page* compact disc, musical products were issued. Whatever his words imply the song makes it clear that Robert Plant wants to be with God.[2]

It seems Page saved all of his smiles and spunkiness for his European dates. On stage in Prague, Czechoslovakia and Efurt, Germany he was seen as cheerful and even in a good mood. Being able to see his girlfriend after each show was, undoubtedly, the source of all of this happiness. He even dashed the communist worker uniform (black garb) for one night in Glasgow, Scotland, upon which date he wore a dark sweater with yellow dragon embroidery. It will be delightful for fans of Page and Plant, maybe even for the two guys themselves, when they finalise another divorce and team up for tours with other people now that every eighteen year old in the universe, who wanted to, has caught up with their act. Page could link with an Italian opera singer, Madonna perhaps, and Plant could team up with any number of feral, WASP guitarists. Personally, I would like to thank them for their subsequent performance in Las Vegas in 1998.

I must leave you now, so I will depart as they left me that night in September, with a feeling from their wildly Romantic and hypnotic, five minute song, 'Whole Lotta Love'. The guitar sounds of Page zoom into audible focus with a steady and fairly rapid succession of B, D and E notes. I am sure that the power of this song will never be equalled, the depth of the vocals, the power in the drum beats and the dark, rhythmic guitar. And so before I return to my own tacet chords, I will say there are only a few rock musicians who can set the emotional tone that Sir Page does in performance. One who comes to my mind as significant is Keith Richard. Think: 'Wild Horses', 'Love Is

Strong', 'Anybody Seen My Baby', 'Angie' and 'Lowdown'. The exceedingly enormous repertoire of Elton John is a pleasure to listen to, but still nothing seems to come close to the simulated lurking at the bottom of the ocean of a Page–Plant song such as 'Most High'. For me 'Whole Lotta Love' is the only midnight lullaby that services my needs. Some have said that familiarity breeds contempt, but my education in the rhythm of James Page only left me needing more guitar notes played by him. As for the scarcity of words in this book, you must understand I am in a hurry to return to the music I have been away from for so long now. To Page in performance; as he plays he relaxes in between the spaces on the frets of his guitar. Every performance is shades different from a previous night's show. He gets the feeling into the music and to the audience in different ways and sometimes he diverts from his original chord structures. Fans sometimes interpret these diversions as errors and sometimes Page himself fears he has made a mistake. Purple lights eerie their way through our vision. Then we cringe as we see hired hand and keyboard player Phillip Andrews play various mandolin parts during the concert. We are tense because Charlie Jones and Phillip Andrews have replaced John Paul Jones, but the show goes on and the flood of music eases our preconceived notions. The sound of the wah-wah pedal in combination with the sound of the guitar solo performed by Jimmy Page eclipses all. Forget the violin bow stunt and forget the fact that Sir Page never verbalises a conversation with an audience. Try to remember the thirty years of communications he made with his guitars and never forget to let the sun shine in.

Bibliography and Works Consulted

Beedell, AV, *Decline of the English Musicians 1788–1888 A Family of English Musicians in Ireland, England, Mauritius and Australia*, USA, Oxford University Press, 1992

Bloom, Allan, *The Closing of the American Mind*, 1987

Bragg, Melvyn, *Speak For England: An Oral History of England: 1900–1975*, 1976

Charters, Robert Johnson Samuel, Oak Publications, New York, 1973

Chilton, John, *Billie's Blues: The Billie Holiday Story*, 1975

Clarke, Donald, *The Rise and Fall of Popular Music*

Clarke, Donald, *Wishing on the Moon: The Life and Times of Billie Holiday*, 1994

Clinton, Susan Maloney, *Cornerstones of Freedom Live Aid*, 1993

Copeland, Ian, *Wild Thing*, 1995

Editors of *Rolling Stone*, *Neil Young, The Rolling Stone Files*, 1994

Electric Guitars and Basses, A Photographic History, Grunn & Carter, 1994

Ellis, Peter Berresford, *The Druids*, 1994

Encyclopaedia Britannica, Chicago London Toronto, 1956

Entertainment Weekly, January 1982

Faithfull, Marianne, *An Autobiography*, 1994

Friedlander, Paul, *Rock and Roll: A Social History*, 1994

Gardner, Helen, *The Metaphysical Poets*, 1985, p.240

Gardner, Helen, *The New Oxford Book of English Verse*, 1972, pp.255, 335

Henderson, David, *'Scuse Me While I Kiss the Sky: The Life of Jimi Hendrix*, 1983

Heylin, Clinton (ed), *The Penguin Book of Rock and Roll Writing*, 1992

Kerman, Joseph, *Listen* (second brief edition), 1992

Lewis, Dave and Pallett, Simon, *Led Zeppelin: The Concert File*, 1997

Lomax, Alan, *The Land Where The Blues Began*, 1993

Plantinga, Leon, *Romantic Music A History of Musical Style of Nineteenth Century Europe*, 1984

Pollock, Bruce, *Hipper Than Our Kids*, 1993, p.186

Rolling Stone, 20th May, 1976, no.213, 2nd June, 1977, no.240, 4th October, 1979, no.301, 18th October, 1979, no.302, 19th January, 1984, no.413, 4th July, 1985 no.451, 4th Sept, 1997, no.768 p.20

Sadie, Stanley (ed), *The New Grove Dictionary of Music and Musicians*, Macmillan Publishers Ltd, London, 1980

Schumacher, Michael, *Crossroads, The Life and Music of Eric Clapton*, 1995, p.56

Shaughnessy, Mary Alice, *Les Paul, An American Original*, 1993

Specht, Richard, *Giacomo Puccini; The Man, His Life, His Work*, 1933

Stone, Irving, *The Agony and the Ecstasy*, 1961

Stukely, William, *Stonehenge: A Temple Restored to the British Druids*, 177?

Swanson, Jim, *The Late Romantic Era*, 1991

Szatmary, David P, *Rockin in Time: A Social History of Rock and Roll*, 1987

The Fellowship of the Ring: Notes on the Text, Houghton Mifflin, 1987

The Great Romantics Selected Poems, Quality Paperback Book Club, 1993, p.957

The New Grove Dictionary of Musical Instruments

Tolkien, J R R, *The Fellowship of the Ring*, 1982

Yorke, Ritchie, *The Led Zeppelin Biography*, Great Britain, Sphere Books Ltd, 1974

1995 Page–Plant American Tour Dates

From *Amusement Business*, 30th January, 1995, vol.107, no.5, p.9

February 26	Pensacola, Florida
February 28	The Omni in Atlanta, Georgia
March 3	Boling Arena in Knoxville, Tennessee
March 4	The Pyramid in Memphis, Tennessee
March 6	Miami Arena in Miami, Florida
March 7	Orlando, Florida
March 10	Kieter Uno Arena
March 13	Erwin Center in Austin, Texas
March 14	The Summit in Houston, Texas
March 16	Barton Coliseum in Little Rock Arkansas
March 18	Dallas Reunion Arena
March 22	USAIR Arena in Landover, Maryland
March 25	Pittsburgh Civic Arena
March 27	Sky Tent Toronto, Canada
March 28	Gund Arena in Cleveland, Ohio
March 31	The Palace of Auburn Hills in Auburn Hills, Michigan
April 3	Correstates at Philadelphia
April 6	Meadowlands Arena in East Rutherford, New Jersey
April 9	Boston Garden in Boston Massachusetts
April 25	Riverfront Coliseum, Cincinatti, Ohio
April 26	Market Square Arena in Indianapolis, Indiana
April 28	Rosemont Horizon in Rosemont, Illinois
May 1	Bradley Center in Milwaukee, Wisconsin

May 2	Target Center in Minneapolis, Minnesota
May 5	Kemper Arena in Kansa City, Missouri
May 6	Keil Center in St. Louis, Missouri
May 8	McNichols Arena in Denver, Colorado
May 10	Delta Center in Salt Lake City, Utah
May 12	MGM Grand Garden Las Vegas, Nevada
May 13	Sports Arena in San Diego, California
May 16 & 17	The Great Western Forum in Inglewood, California
May 19	Oakland, California
May 20	San Jose Arena
May 25	Pacific Coliseum in Tacoma, Washington

In June their European tour began and in October, American tour dates resumed. In October, Page and Plant were at Madison Square Garden for two nights. The band toured Russia and Japan at this time and their world tour concluded on 28th February, 1996.

1998 Page–Plant Tour

February 21	Zagreb, Croatia, Dom Sportova
February 23	Budapest, Hungary, Sports Hall
February 25	Prague, Czechoslovakia
February 26	Katowice, Poland, Spodek Auditorium
February 27	San Remo, Italy (Italian television show)
March 1	Bucharest Romania
March 2	Sofia, Bulgaria, Palace of Culture
March 5 & 6	Istanbul, Turkey, Bostanci Center
March 25	London, England, Shepherd's Bush Empire
March 26	*Top of the Pops*, London, England, Elstree Studios
March 27	*TFI Friday*, London, England, Riverside Studios
March 30	Paris, France, La Cigale
March 31	Canal, France
May 5	London, England, White City
May 19	Pensacola, Florida, Civic Center
May 20	Tampa, Florida, Ice Palace
May 22	Miami, Florida, Civic Center
May 23	Jacksonville, Florida, Coliseum
May 26	Charlotte, NC, Coliseum
May 27	Charleston, South Carolina
May 29	Atlanta, GA, Lakewood Amphitheater
May 30	Tupelo, MS, Tupelo Coliseum
June 1	Birmingham, Alabama, Civic Center
June 2	Nashville, Tennessee, Coliseum
June 4	Oklahoma City, OK, Myriad (I attended this one)

June 6	Kansas City, MO, Kemper Arena
June 7	St Louis, MO, Keil Center
June 9	Indianapolis, IN, Market Square
June 10	Milwaukee, WI, Bradley Center
June 12	Minneapolis, MN, Target Center
June 13	Fargo, SD, Fargodome
June 15 &16	Chicago, IL, United Center
June 26 & 27	Detroit, Michigan, Palace of Auber Hills
June 29	Grand Rapids, MI, Van Andel arena
July 1	Pittsburgh, PA, Civic Center
July 3	Cleveland, Ohio, Gund Arena
July 4	Toronto, Ontario, Molson Ampitheater
July 7	Washington, DC, MCI Center
July 8	Virginia Beach, VA, Ampitheatre
July 10	Philadelphia, PA, Correstates
July 11	Albany, New York
July 13	Boston, Massachusetts, Fleet Center
July 14	Great Woods, Mansfield, Massachusetts
July 16	New York, NY, Madison Square Garden
July 18	East Rutherford, New Jersey
July 19	Long Island, New York, Jones Beach Theatre
August 21	Vaduz, Switzerland, The Little Big One Festival (attendance: 5,000), they played outdoors in rain
August 23	Bizzare Festival, near Cologne, Germany (rain)
August 26	Dublin, Ireland, The Point
August 29	Reading Festival, London, England
September 5	Vancouver, BC
September 6	Seattle, WA, The Gorge (attendance: 20,000)
September 8	Portland, Oregon, Rose Garden
September 9	Boise, ID
September 11	San Francisco, CA Concord Pavilion

September 12	Mountain View, CA, Shoreline Amphitheatre
September 16	Red Rocks, Denver, Colorado
September 17	San Jose, CA
September 18	Los Angeles, CA, Irvine Meadows Amphitheatre
September 19	Hollywood, CA, Hollywood Bowl
September 21	San Diego, CA
September 23	Las Vegas, NV, MGM Grand Garden (I saw this date also)
September 24	Phoenix, AZ, American West Arena
September 26	San Antonio, TX
September 27	Dallas, TX
September 30	Houston, TX, Cynthia Woods Mitchell Pavilion
October 1	New Orleans, LA (live radio broadcast to all fifty states)
October 2	Memphis, TN, Pyramid
October 30	University of London, London, England (attendance: 500)
November 2	Glasgow, Scotland, SECC (attendance: 8,000)
November 3	Manchester, England, *Manchester Evening News* Arena
November 5&6	Wembley Arena, London, England
November 9	Rennes, France, Liberté (attendance: 4,000)
November 10	Paris, France, Bercy (attendance: 15,000)
November 12	Zagreb, Croatia, (attendance: 5,000)
November 13	Vienna, Austria, Stadthalle (attendance: 10,000)
November 16	Erfurt, Germany, Messehalle (attendance: 11,000)
November 17	Prague, Czech Republic, Sports Hall
November 19	Milan, Italy, Forum

November 20	Zurich, Switzerland, Hallenstadion
November 23	Munich, Germany, Olympiahalle
November 25	Montpelier, France, Zenith
November 26	Bordeaux, France, Patinoire
November 28	Toulon, France, Zenith
November 29	Lyon, France, Halle Tony Garnier
December 1	Ghent, Belgium, Exhibition Hall, Flanders Expo
December 2	Oberhausen, Germany
December 3	Frankfurt, Germany, Festhalle

Led Zeppelin's Bootlegged Recordings

(Only the last of these manufacturers had the band's permission to tape their music – on the 1995 tour Page and Plant allowed tapers a special seating section at their shows)

A Secret History
Absence/Toasted – Led Zeppelin onstage in Europe in 1975
Archipelago
Ballcrusher
BBC Broadcast – Royal Albert Hall, 1971
Bath, 1970
BBC Zep – 1971
Best of Led Zeppelin Live in Concert
Blueberry Hill – Los Angeles Forum, 4th September, 1970
Blueberry Hill
Bonzo's Birthday Party, 31st May, 1973
Caution Explosive – *Winterland*, San Francisco 1969 and Los Angeles 1970
Days of Heaven – The Empire, Liverpool, UK, 14th January, 1973
The Destroyer/Smilin – 28th April, 1977
Detroit – Just About Back
For Badge Holders Only
Flying High/White Knight
Front Row
Going to California – Berkley
Hiawatha Express
Jennings Farm Blues
Jim's Picks
Knebworth Fair Vol.I, 4th August, 1979

Knebworth Fair Vol.II, 11th August, 1979
Knebworth 79
Knebworth Vol.I
Knebworth Vol.II, 11th August, 1979
Lead Set
Led Zeppelin III
Led Zeppelin/Joker
Led Zeppelin – Stockholm 1968/1969
Listen to This Eddie
Loove!
Magical Mystery Tape
Melbourne Madness
Mudslide – 1971 Radio Broadcast
My Brain Hurts – Japan, December, 1972
No Quarter – Earl's Court, London, England 18th May, 1975
Olympic Gold
Rock Hour
Royal Albert Hall
Sin City Social – Inglewood Forum 31st May, 1973 and 3rd June, 1973
Stairway to Heaven 25th June, 1975
Studio Daze
Smoke Gets In Your Eyes
Swiss Made – Zurich, Switzerland, 1979
Tight But Loose
Trampled Underfoot – Madison Square Garden, 1975
VooDoo Drive
Walk Don't Run
White Summer – Hamburg, Germany, 11th March, 1970
We're Gonna Groove, Shoreline Arena in Mountain View, California, 7th October, 1995

Discography for Led Zeppelin

Led Zeppelin 1969
Led Zeppelin II 1969
Led Zeppelin III 1970
Untitled 1971
Houses of The Holy 1973
Physical Graffiti 1975
Presence 1976
The Song Remains The Same 1976
In Through The Out Door 1979
Coda 1982
Led Zeppelin Remasters (a boxed CD set) 1990

Jimmy Page Discography
(outside Led Zeppelin)

Little Games (A Yardbirds Gem) 1967
The Honey Drippers Vol.I 1984
The Original Soundtrack, Death Wish II 1982

Jimmy's Back Pages

Will & The Poor Boys with Bill Wyman 1985
The Firm 1985
Mean Business 1986
Outrider 1988
Coverdale Page 1993

The Adventures of Page and Plant in the 1990s

No Quarter 1994
Led Zeppelin BBC Sessions 1997
Walking Into Clarksdale 1998

1999 Live Performances of Jimmy Page

June 27	London Charity Concert with The Black Crowes (Café du Paris)
October 9	Net Aid Benefit Concert (Rutherford, New Jersey)
October 12, 13, 14	Roseland Ballroom, New York (The Black Crowes)
October 16	Worchester, MA (with The Black Crowes)
October 18, 19	Greek Theatre, Los Angeles (with The Black Crowes)

Sources and Notes

Sustain

[1] Shirley, Ralph, *Occultists and Mystics of All Ages*, The Citadel Press Secaucus, New Jersey, 1974, p.94.

[2] Ewen, David, *The Home Book of Musical Knowledge*.

[3] The Great Romantics, *Hyperion: A Fragment*, New York, Quality Paperback Book Club, 1993, p.954.

Winter

[1] Routh, Francis, *Contemporary British Music: The 25 Years from 1945 to 1970*.

[2] Routh, Francis, *Contemporary British Music: The 25 Years from 1995 to 1997*.

[3] Mylett, Howard, *Jimmy Page: Tangents Within A Framework*. Thanks go to Mr Mylett for the knowledge of Page's mother's name and for confirmation of his father's name. I somehow always knew that the father of Jimmy Page would share the same name.

[4] A Scottish singer acquaintance of mine, Brian O'Shea, sang on the 1970 LP, *Sutch and Friends*.

[5] Brian O'Shea.

[6] *Rock and Roll*, produced by WGBH, Boston, BBC, 1995.

[7] Oakley, Giles, *The Devil's Music: A History of the Blues*, BBC, Great Britain, 1976, p.195.

[8] Grasse, Jesse, *Guitar Player*, August 1993, p.75. The author gives a wonderful description of influences on Jimmy Page and describes in which songs these surface in an article titled 'Zeppelinage'.

[9] *Rock and Roll* (series of five video cassettes), produced by WGBH, Boston, BBC, 1995, Episode 5: Crossroads.

Pressed for Time

[1] The Great Romantics, *Selected Poems, Lord Byron, Percy Bysshe Shelley, John Keats*, New York, Quality Paperback Book Club, 1993.

[2] Smithsonian, January 1997, p.20, displayed the upgraded Fender and Les Paul model guitars.

Amber in Starlight

[1] Welch, Chris, *Led Zeppelin – Dazed and Confused*, London, 1998.

Thunderous Strength in Stargroves and Stadiums

[1] The Great Romantics, *Selected Poems, Lord Byron, Percy Bysshe Shelley, John Keats*, New York, Quality Paperback Book Club, 1993.

[2] Maslin, Janet, 'Zeppelin Flies', *Newsweek*, 20th June, 1977.

[3] I have listened to Led Zeppelin records to maintain a perspective on their music.

[4] *Speak for England: An Oral History of England – 1900–1975*. Based on interviews with the inhabitants of Wigton, Cumberland, this is the best book I have found to set the tone for the world wars and to tell the stories of people who lived in England during the 1940s.

[5] Cole, Richard, *Stairway to Heaven*. This is responsible for my knowledge of the birthplace of Jimmy Page.

[6] *The Times*, London, 2nd January, 1967, p.65.

[7] *Rock and Roll* (series of five video cassettes), produced by WGBH, Boston, BBC, 1995, Episode 5: Crossroads

[8] *Crawdaddy*, June, 1975.

[9] Anderson, Christopher, *Jagger Unauthorized*, New York, Delacourte Press, 1993.

[10] Tolinski, Brad and Di Benedetto, Greg, 'Pride and Joys', *Guitar World*, May 1993, p.52.

[11] *Rolling Stone*, 4th July, 1985, no.415.

[12] Pollock, Bruce, *Hipper Than Our Kids*, 1993, p.186. Jeopardy question aired on 6th September, 1997. The answer was: 'What is a zeppelin?'

Adventurous Souls

[1] Interview Page had with *Trouser Press* in 1997 with David Schulps.

[2] *Rolling Stone*, 20th May, 1976, No.213, p.64.

[3] Anderson, Christopher, *Jagger Unauthorized*, New York, Delacourte Press, 1993.

[4] *People*, 27th August, 1976, p.32.

[5] Martinson, Thomas H, *ARCO Everything You Need To Know To Score High on the GRE*, Simon & Schuster, 1997.

The Business

[1] Frazer, James, *The Goldon Bough*, 3rd Edition, New York, MacMillan Publishing, 1950.

[2] Giuliano, Geoffrey, *Behind Blue Eyes: The Life of Pete Townshend*, p.25.

[3] Des Barres, Pamela, *I'm With the Band: Confessions of a Groupie*, p.185.

[4] Clarke, BFL, *Church Builders of the Nineteenth Century: A Study of the Gothic Revival in England*, Augustus M Kelley, New York, 1969.

[5] Goodman, Fred, *The Mansion on the Hill. Dylan, Young, Geffen, Springsteen and the Head-on Collision of Rock and Commerce*, Vintage Press, p.305.

Symphonies, Melodies and the Love Music of my Life

[1] The Great Romantics, *Selected Poems, Lord Byron, Percy Bysshe Shelley, John Keats*, New York, Quality Paperback Book Club, 1993.

[2] *Biography* magazine, August 1998, p.14.

[3] Obrecht, Jas (ed), *Guitar Player*, 'Blues Guitar: The Men Who Made the Music', 1993, pp.106–112.

[4] *Vanity Fair*, 14th September, 1988. A review of a performance Jimmy Page gave at the Knight Center in Miami, Florida.

[5] Yorke, Ritchie, *Led Zeppelin: The Definitive Biography*, p.162. According to Yorke and his sources and observations, Page was using cocaine in 1973. On p.246 of his book he tells about a time in 1982 when Page was charged for possession of cocaine and he describes Peter Grant was having a problem with dependency on heroin at this time. On p.249 Page is said to be quitting his heroin use after the ARMS benefit performance (good news).

The Absolute Best

[1] *The World Almanac and Book of Facts 1984*, Funk and Wagnalls Corp, p.316.

[2] Tolinski, Brad, 'David and Goliath', *Guitar World*, May 1993.

Rolling Stone, 4th September, 1997, no.768, p.20.

Guitar Player, January 1992, p.88.

Guitar Player, January 1984, p.94.

Guitar World, May 1993, p.52.

Friedlander, Paul, *Rock and Roll, A Social History*, p.242.

Schumacher, Michael, *Crossroads: The Life and Music of Eric Clapton*, p.56.

Community

[1] I Ching

[2] Giuliano, Geoffrey, *Dark Horse: The Private Life of George Harrison*, 1990.

[3] *People Weekly*, July 1985.

[4] *Guitar Player*, January 1984, p.94.

[5] *Rolling Stone*, 19th January, 1984, no.413, p.20.

[6] From the Internet: www.ripon.edu/Students/Quickr/jpport.text.

Cultural Curves

[1] *Entertainment Weekly*, 3rd February, 1995, p.12.

[2] Ellis, Beresford, Peter, The Druids, Grand Rapids, Michigan, William B. Eerdmans Publishing Co., 1994.

[3] Love, Robert (ed), *The Best of Rolling Stone: 25 Years of Journalism on the Edge*.

Palmer, Robert, *Up the Mountain*, p.25.

Cadence

[1] *Webster's Ninth New Collegiate Dictionary*, 1983, p.163.

[2] Patowski, Joe Nick and Crawford, Bill, *Stevie Ray Vaughan: Caught in the Crossfire*, 1993.

[3] George, Nelson, *The Death of Rhythm and Blues*, p.110.

[4] Whitburn, Joel (ed), *The Billboard Book of Top 40 Hits*, sixth edition, p.440. Most of Ms Nicks recording career is documented here.

[5] *Guitar Player*, August 1993, p.75; *Guitar Player*, November 1992, p.96 – a review of Little Games.

[6] *Rolling Stone*, 4th July, 1985, no.451, p.32.

[7] Charters, Samuel, *Robert Johnson*, 1973, p.81.

[8] Bloom, Allan, *The Closing of the American Mind*, 1987, p.79.

Content and Style

[1] *Guitar Player*, January 1982, p.88.

[2] *Guitar Player*, January 1984, p.94.

[3] Tolinski, Brad, 'David and Goliath', *Guitar World*, May 1993, p.46.

Billboard, 5th March, Vol. CVI, no.10, p.12.

Autumn Garland

[1] Information concerning the 6th August wedding performance and August tour dates came from Dave Linwood's Tight But Loose website on the Internet: www.linwood.demon.co.uk.

The Economy of Listening

[1] From the Internet on 23rd March, 1998:
www.ripon.edu/ Students/Quick/jpport.text.
The Decline of the English Musician 1788–1888, p.82.

The Making of a Hit Record

[1] *Music, An Illustrated History*, Hamlyn Publishing, 1986, p.137.

[2] *Hit Parader*, March 1998, no.402, p.56.

[3] *Top*, April 1998, p.17.

[4] Whitburn, Joel, *The Billboard Book of Top 40 Hits*, sixth edition, p.473.

[5] Porter, Katherine Anne, *Ship of Fools*, 1945, 1962. Information comes from the page which prefaces her story.

[6] Pennick, Nigel, *Celtic Saints: An Illustrated and Authoritative Guide to these Extraordinary Men and Women*, p.20.

Remains of the Day

[1] The interview between Page and Rodgers was conducted over the telephone which Page was in Vancouver, BC and appeared in the 20th September, 1998 edition of The Arizona Republic.

[2] Photo of Plant with Tori Amos is in 12th November, 1998, no.799 of Rolling Stone.

1998 tour dates came courtesy of David Linwood's Internet site: Tight but Loose: www.linwood.demon.co.uk.

I snapped the photo of Page with his Gibson Sunburst on 23rd September, 1998 at the MGM.

The photo of Led Zeppelin was taken by Richard Falzone on 27th June in Nurnburg, Germany.